STARBORN

JESSE TIMM

LODESTAR SAGA
BOOK 01

This book is dedicated
to Trevor, for his excellent editing,
to McKayla, for her endless support,
and to all my friends
who helped me to reach this goal.
You are the real heroes.

TABLE OF CONTENTS

PROLOGUE
FALLING FROM HEAVEN

Joseph, Oregon
July 28, 2027

"It's quite incredible, Doctor Holst," the young scientist said over a video call, looking into the wizened face of his mentor displayed on his computer screen. "The samples I've collected are displaying properties I've never seen before. The meteor showers are absolutely phenomenal as well. They seem to burn a greenish-blue, which might imply the presence of copper sulfates and chlorides, but... well, I suppose you'll see when I visit soon."

"Ah, yes, I look forward to it, Soren," the silver-haired, bespectacled elder replied. "Retirement has not been kind. Some research and company would be welcome."

"Then you should be happy to know that I will begin my road trip first thing tomorrow morning."

"Road trip?! You're planning to drive all the way

from Oregon to Virginia?!" Holst's eyes were wide.

"Unfortunately, the lab doesn't want to pay for a private flight again, and trying to bring radioactive material on a commercial flight would raise too many eyebrows, no matter what my credentials may be. So driving it is."

"Perhaps I could convince them otherwise," Holst offered, his tone mildly defiant.

"By the time you get them to agree, you'll be blue in the face and I could have already made it there and back three times." When Holst opened his mouth to argue, Soren cut him off. "It's fine, Doctor, really. I'm perfectly capable of making the drive."

The doctor looked slightly taken aback, but digressed. "Ah, well, in that case... drive safe, my friend."

"I will, Doctor. Stay well until I get there."

"Oh, no need to worry about me. I'm fit as an ox. Good night, Soren."

"Good night, Doctor."

The young man closed the laptop he had been using for the call and strode to his study's window. Nautical twilight had left the yard beyond in darkness. A digital clock on his desk told him it was 9:52 P.M.

Outside, another meteor shower had begun to fall. That would make for the third in a week. As with the last two, emerald and cobalt streaks trailed behind the falling space rocks. Occasionally, one would break apart, splitting the viridian-colored blurs into smaller gashes of light to rend the otherwise black sky. The sight could be topped by little else in the known world. The northern lights might outshine them to the untrained eye, but to someone with the expertise of Doctor Soren Grant, they were in a league all their own.

Doctor Grant made his way out of his house and onto his back porch to enjoy the spectacle. Though he had witnessed the last two just the same, it wasn't a sight that could grow old or repetitive yet—not to him. Hundreds of lights— seemingly small from this distance, but in reality, each many meters in diameter—cast a faint illumination on the space-themed lawn ornaments that dotted Soren's backyard.

Samples he had collected were home to a

metal whose exact composition the Earth had not seen before. It had properties of beta radiation akin to tritium, but it possessed a sheen and magnetism most closely matching copper or even iron. Soren's hypothesis: this combination of properties may have somehow loaned to the unusual coloration of the rocks' blazing tails.

While admiring the airborne display, the scientist was blindsided in an instant. Meteors fall quickly, hurtling at thousands of miles per hour toward Earth's surface. And one just so happened to be large enough to make it to the ground without bursting or burning up prematurely. The impact shook Soren's house before he knew what was happening; he had no chance to escape the ensuing explosion of brilliantly colored flames and debris. The radioactive chunk of extraterrestrial minerals smashed the scientist's house, sending wood and brick skyward. The tremors caused the decorated lawn to topple its own ornaments. And the young man was launched across his yard as everything he owned was turned into a crater.

For Soren, the world went black. Blistering heat was succeeded by rigorous cold. He opened his eyes once. Unable to focus, he saw only a blur of whites, and sirens blasted his ears during the small moment he managed to keep himself awake. A second later, his eyes attempted to open again. Lights rose into his vision and left just as quickly.

He couldn't accurately recall anything but a numbing pain after. Ringing filled his ears. The sounds of voices drilled into his head like a migraine. He heard them arguing over if something was possible. The only thing that seemed unlikely to him was a moment of silence. Peace—what was it like again? So quickly he had forgotten.

And so it all slowly faded away. As dark as nothing could get. No lights. No sound.

Nothing.

And at 2:33 A.M., Soren Grant's vital signs vanished.

CHAPTER 01
BIRTH OF A NOVA

Secret U.S. Military Base
July 31, 2027

He awoke slowly, taking in his surroundings. A blank, dull gray room surrounded him. A painfully bright light shone above him. He laid not on a bed, but on a hard concrete floor. His bones and muscles ached. He wasn't entirely sure what had happened to get him to this moment. So much was a blur at this point, his thoughts and memories disconnected and misaligned. He felt strange somehow. Feverish, yet energetic. His head pulsed with splitting pain.

Then, a voice broke the echoing silence, "You're finally awake, Doctor Grant." What had at first seemed to be a wall faded into a window that looked into another room.

"What's happening?" Soren groggily asked, stumbling to his feet. He squinted against bright lights that caused his head to throb with renewed vigor.

"I'd imagine after being struck with a meteor, you would have questions," a muscular figure with tattooed arms on the other side of the glass answered, standing from the chair he had been relaxed in moments ago. He was garbed in a casual sort of fatigues—camouflage trousers and a faded green tank top—that cued Soren in that he was likely speaking to someone of military rank. "You died three nights ago. Doctors thought it was from radiation poisoning. But what no one can explain is that as your death certificate was being filled out, your vitals came back."

The pounding in Soren's head resulted in him taking a moment longer than normal to process what he was being told. "Wait, wait, wait... What?" Soren stammered. "So I died... and came back to life somehow? And all on my own?" He took another couple of moments pondering this. "Despite the improbability of that actually happening, I'll bite. So why does that justify me being held in an interrogation chamber?" He began to realize that his current garb was adding to the light reflecting into his eyes, and was the source of a horrible crunching sound every time he moved. "And why am I wearing tin foil? And... am I glowing?"

"One at a time, Doctor," the man coaxed, raising a large hand to gesture for Soren to calm down. "The outfit is actually a special weave of tin and tungsten designed to keep radiation at bay. It and the room are to contain the energy that is creating the glow. You see, when you returned to life, you became blisteringly hot. Much of your surroundings went up in flames. Not to mention the radiation you've given off. We had to find a way to keep this energy from harming anything further."

Soren did his best to follow, but the science didn't seem to add up. Nevertheless, the military man continued, "Luckily, the radiation, if the reports are true, primarily consists of ultraviolet and electromagnetic energy. Nothing particularly harmful in small quantities. Almost like—"

"The sunlight that reaches the earth," Soren concluded, finishing the man's sentence. Finally, something made at least some sense. "So if I get too close to someone, they would effectively get a sunburn, if I'm understanding you correctly."

"Effectively, yes," the man said with mild irritation at having been cut off. "The thing is, we don't know for sure how it works. It showed up out of nowhere, and it has certainly diminished significantly since. But if it were to spike again, it could be catastrophic.

"To give you a sense of scale," he continued, "a few of the personnel here were wagering that you might have been giving off enough energy at first to power a city. Some even gambled harvesting that energy for an hour could have powered NYC for a week. The jury's still out on that for sure until the tests are finished, but whether true or false, the energy levels were unprecedented."

"Excuse me," Soren interjected again, his headache coming in slower waves as time progressed. "If we're going to make this an extended conversation, it's probably best that I learn what to call you. You clearly know who I am already."

"Command Sergeant Major Harold Bolton. Served in the Middle East for—wait, how did you just do that?" The man jumped back in astonishment.

Soren had been focusing for a while on the energy he was giving off, and had just managed to contain it within himself, stopping the glow he had been projecting. The side effect was a greater pain in his skull. "Seems I can control this radiation with a bit of focus, Sergeant," he explained through gritted teeth. "Makes the migraine near unbearable, though."

"That's Command Sergeant Major to you. Now— what the hell?!" Bolton suddenly shielded his eyes from what was now before him.

Soren had this time pushed the energy out from himself, creating a much brighter glow than before. And the pain faded back, letting him think more clearly. Soren let a sigh of relief. "Better out than in, it seems," he chuckled. "You're not wrong. I have a lot of this energy trapped inside me. But with a little knowledge of physics, I should be able to…" Soren trailed off. Then, with his eyes closed and his face a bit scrunched, he began to focus the energy slowly toward his feet, and to his and Bolton's amazement, he began to generate lift, hovering a few inches above the ground.

"I'll be damned! Looks like you *can* control it."

"So does that give me any chance of being let out of this petri dish?" Soren asked, still hovering. "I'm used to being the one doing the experiments, not the one being experimented on."

"If you think we're going to let a man who could possibly be the personification of nuclear fallout walk around, you—"

"Right," Soren cut him off. Now that he had diminished the pain that had plagued his skull, his mind was racing. "Look, no offense, but you haven't been the most consistent with your story. That said, with the information you've given me, I've got some tests I need to run. I'm a scientist—it's what I do. I did ask nicely, and it seems you aren't too willing to do things the easy way. So if you'll excuse me..."

"Now just you hold on a mi—THE HELL ARE YOU DOING?!" Bolton's demeanor jumped from mild agitation to outright ferocity in nanoseconds, and it wasn't hard to see why.

Soren had flown himself to just high enough to be able to press his hands to the ceiling. He channeled energy to his hands and began heating the concrete to the point that it glassed. "I figure, with wanting to keep me 'contained,' as you say, you'd have me in some isolated bunker. I don't know how many layers of concrete there might be between me and the outside world, and frankly, I don't care. I'm getting out of here." As he finished his statement, the now-glassed concrete above him began shattering, sending superheated shrapnel flying.

Small bits of glass and concrete rained on Soren from above, yet they only popped and were launched with renewed vigor as they met his hot skin. Somehow, even though Soren knew he might easily be raising the temperature around him hundreds of degrees, he still felt oddly comfortable. In fact, it seemed that the hotter he got, the better he felt. With increasing force and energy, the concrete broke apart more readily, and Soren slowly gained more altitude.

The glowing, exploding glass that burst as it met his skin gave Soren the appearance of a firework display, oddly fitting of the excitement he felt at escaping and studying the strange powers he now found himself in possession of. And he noticed in that moment that the glow coming off his skin seemed to match that of the burning meteors. More to research later, which only heightened his excitement.

"We've got a breach!" Bolton yelled into a radio. "All personnel prepare to intercept! Test Subject Quasar is escaping! Repeat, Test Subject Quasar is escaping!"

As the chiseled man began calling for backup, Soren had already burrowed up to half his height in the concrete all in a matter of seconds, and getting faster as he pressed further. "Quasar, huh?" he muttered to himself. "I'll have to remember that one." It took nearly all of his focus to push the energy in the right directions, especially in the right proportions for keeping upward momentum, and the small time it took to listen to what Bolton was saying meant he temporarily lost his balance. Luckily, on noticing his deviation from course, he was able to quickly correct his energy outputs, and within another minute of sparking like a human-sized welding torch, he burst into the outside world.

He was somewhere in a desert. Nevada was

his best guess. As he heard a helicopter taking off from the base now a few hundred yards below him, he darted off to the north. The chopper was quick to follow, but of course, Doctor Grant was learning further extents of his power as he experimented.

"Doctor Grant!" Bolton's voice echoed through a megaphone. "Return to the ground and surrender yourself immediately, or we will have to resort to lethal force! This is your only warning!"

Soren ignored the military officer's proclamation and continued on his course, and Bolton fulfilled on his promise. Bullets began to fly his way, narrowly missing a few times. Soren quickly circled the chopper, taunting as he passed around it. Then he dropped toward the ground and resumed his trajectory to the north at a much faster pace than before. The aircraft was no match for the speeds Soren could reach as he began to push his powers to their limits.

The chopper tried to give chase, but its target was much too fast. As Bolton watched the glowing man disappear into the horizon, he cursed under his breath. "Dammit. That guy's sure got balls pulling that stunt. We'll return to base for now. President Sharpe will want to hear about this."

Owyhee, Nevada
July 31, 2027

Soren put down in a mostly empty field near a gas station with a sign that read "DUCK VALLEY GAS -N- GO." It was a short walk over to the station, where he found someone outside preoccupied with fueling a rusted pickup truck. "Hey," Soren hailed.

"Hey, there," the man responded, not looking to the source of the voice yet.

"If you don't mind my asking, where exactly am I?"

"How does one end up passing through a Native American Reservation without—wait, what's with the getup?" he cut himself off when he, at last, looked in Soren's direction.

"Hey, now, I thought I was the one asking

questions."

"Right. Guess you must be one of them sci-fi convention weirdos. Anyhoo, you're thereabouts of Owyhee, Nevada. Just about on the Idaho border."

"So northwest would take me to Oregon."

"Yep."

"Thanks," Soren replied, beginning to walk away from the station.

"Wait, buddy," the man called after him. "You need a ride somewhere?"

"No need," Soren explained, hovering a bit once he was a fair distance from the pumps. The man rubbed his eyes before looking back at the scientist floating about a foot above the ground.

"Holy shit. You're actually flying! Uh… you ain't some alien gonna abduct me are you?"

"Nothing like that," Soren laughed. A car passed by, swerving back into its lane after the driver realized their displacement from staring at the spectacle of the glowing, flying man.

"So… you one of them government experiments you see out here sometimes?"

"That one's complicated. Not entirely sure, myself."

"Sorry, I don't talk to your type often." The man shook his head. "Come on, Jim, you can do this," he muttered to himself. He'd be sweating from nerves, if not for the already present perspiration brought about by the desert's summer heat. "You look human enough. Got a name at least?"

Soren considered the question for a moment, debating whether to use his real name. But his mind stuck on the code name Bolton had used earlier. "How about Quasar?" he decided on, flying off as a woman pulled into the station, stepping out of her car and staring at the blip of green light disappearing into the distance that had been a person just a minute ago.

"First time seeing an alien?" the man with the truck said to the woman, who only nodded, her jaw ajar with awe. "I could tell you some stories."

CHAPTER 02
REMODELING

Joseph, Oregon
Saturday, July 31, 2027

The sun was already setting as the familiar Sacajawea Peak came into view. By the time Soren landed on an outlook above his now ruined house, it was dark. The landscape below was scrambling with military personnel. Spotlights swept the perimeter while ATVs roamed, carrying who-knows-what from place to place.

The space rock samples he had collected before would have likely been destroyed. And if they had somehow survived the impact, they would surely be in government custody by now. Except...there was a safe he kept some money in. And he had stored a single sample inside just in case of a burglary. As long as that safe was still intact, there was a chance he could get the sample.

Of course, there was one major flaw. If

somehow these government goons would be willing to let him back into his house, which was unlikely to begin with, he no longer had his identification to prove who he was. So it would have to be a heist. Get in, grab some of his cash—he was getting hungry and needed to buy food soon—snag the sample, and get out. Ideally, he would get in without alerting too many people. And there was a checkpoint on the perimeter not far from his current perch that had only two guards.

So naturally, he soared down to the checkpoint in question and announced himself. "Hello, there. I come in peace," he waved.

"Who the hell are you?!" the first of two guards shouted as both of them raised their rifles.

The second chimed in, "Stop where you are and put both hands behind your head. Move another inch and we'll shoot."

"Ah," Soren replied. "My apologies, but this *is* my house after all. I just need to grab a couple of things before your men make off with them."

"Are you deaf? I said don't move!" the second uniformed figure commanded.

"Right, right. I guess it's my bad for hoping you'd

do things more calmly," Soren retorted, taking another step toward the men.

"Open fire!" the first man barked out, and the muzzles on the guards' firearms lit up. Soren extended his arms, recalling what Bolton had said about electromagnetic radiation. It would take a lot of it to deter a bullet, but with enough focus perhaps he could pull it off. He channeled the energy through his hands into the area in front of him, projecting a kind of invisible forcefield that hummed with electrical energy and smelled of burning ozone. Bullets curved around Soren even better than he could have predicted, redirected by the magnetic field. Combined with Soren's emitted heat, the bullets dropped to the ground in the form of dripping hot slag in a ring around him.

As the soldiers realized what was happening, they ceased fire. "So, I think I forgot to mention, I'm able to put out magnetic rays. Oh, and I can practically vaporize those bullets with heat, so it seems those guns won't be doing so much as scratching me."

"Backup at Checkpoint Delta! We need backup!" guard number two shouted into his radio.

"Sounds like fun," Soren responded. "Guess that means it's time to split." He rocketed into the air, flying over the guards toward the collapsed wall of the house. He put out a small burst of energy in front of him to blast some of the debris out of his path, and into the house he went.

A group of men in biohazard suits was inside. "Isn't it a bit dangerous in here for you guys? But since you're here, have any of you seen a safe box, no more than two feet in any dimension?"

The people shook their heads, looks of fear, astonishment, and awe on all their faces beyond the protective shields before them.

"Good, that means it should still be in here. Oh, and you may want to evacuate the premises. What's left of this house is going to collapse in on itself soon. And make sure to tell the guys with guns that as well."

As the hazmat crew obediently filed out of the rubble, Soren blasted a hole in the wreckage where the stairs once were. Dropping to the basement, he found the safe just where he remembered it. Soren quickly got it open and pulled out a fair amount of his money and the sample of space rock. Then he flew back upstairs to his closet, grabbed a singed suitcase, and a few articles of dusty, tattered clothing that was in tact enough to still be wearable. Finding his backup cell phone cracked, though still in semi-working order, he stuffed everything into the trunk before burning a hole through the remaining shambles of a roof. As he did so, the walls began crumbling around him, the multiple impacts demolishing what remained of their integrity.

With the suitcase of his belongings in hand, Soren shot out into the open again. Beneath him, the last bits of his house fell to the ground, kicking up more dust and debris. He grimaced. He never expected to lose his house to a meteor, and he doubted he'd have any luck getting insurance to cover "meteor impact" damage. The guards on the ground below him attempted to fire on him, but the dust had left them blind to all but the faintest of light that reached them, and Soren was able to flee completely unharmed.

When the dust settled and it was revealed that their target was gone from the scene, the guards were at a loss. The second of the two who had directly encountered Soren went to the tent in their midst marked with the U.S. Presidential Seal. Outside, he was met by Secret Service officers who allowed him into the tent after a momentary ID scan.

Inside, more Secret Service lined the walls of the oversized tent, while a woman at a makeshift desk spoke to a holographic screen which showed the face of Command Sergeant Major Bolton. "Excuse me a moment, Bolton," she said in a cool voice. "What is it you need, Corporal? I would hope this is some kind of report about the commotion moments ago?" She now addressed the soldier that had shown up in person, her expression indignant.

"I figured you should know, Madam President. A glowing man showed up here just a bit ago and broke into the investigation scene. He claimed to be the original owner of this property." The report he gave, though about an extraordinary event, was offered with as much formality as any report he might normally present to his superiors. "He was in and out in less than a minute. We might have missed him if not for him emitting light."

"Did you see which way he went?"

"He left us mostly blind, Madam President. But to the best of our ability to tell, it would seem he is going east."

"Thank you, Corporal. If that is all, you are dismissed," she waved, turning back to the image of Harold Bolton before her. The corporal filed out of the tent with a salute "Your project came here, it seems. Rather quickly, too. And if he's heading east, our resources say the only contact he has there is a man named Hardwin Holst. I'll be sure you have his information by morning."

"Madam President, if you don't mind me asking, what would *I* need this man's information for?" Harold asked.

"Because," she replied, lowering her voice, "I am authorizing you to use the Star Buster Beta Mk-III. Catch this man. I would prefer him to be brought back alive. But if you cannot contain him, then perhaps it is best that he is destroyed. If what you've told me is true, him roaming may be dangerous to the people of this country. Especially if he has malicious intent."

"Th-the Star Buster?" Bolton's composure

seemed to have crumbled slightly at the mention of it.

"Is there a problem?" the President asked, half turned away, her eyebrow raised.

"Not at all, Madam President. I will make you and this country proud. By your leave."

As the hologram vanished, the woman sat quietly for a moment. "I hope you do, Bolton," she said into nothingness. "For the safety of us all."

Springfield, Missouri
Sunday, August 01, 2027

It was dawn when Soren touched down again in Springfield, Missouri. Finding a building atop which few would be able to see him, he was able to change his clothes. By this point, the growling in his stomach had become unbearable.

Flying around the city for a short time, he was able to find a place for takeout: Hurts Donut Company. After ordering a handful of maple bacon bars, Soren rocketed to the roof where he was able to sit and eat his newly acquired and rather tasty breakfast.

When his hunger was sated, he reached into his suitcase to find the cracked, nearly dead phone. It had just enough juice for one short call, so he dialed the person he needed to speak to most.

"Hello?" came the answer from the other end of the line.

"Doctor Holst? It's me, Soren."

"Soren?! I heard you were dead! What happened?"

"I don't have a lot of time before my phone dies, and believe me: it's a long story. I'm on my way in your direction, but do you know of anywhere near the Kentucky-Virginia line that you'd be willing to meet up with me? It's kind of urgent."

There was a short moment of silence while the old man thought. "Hmm... if you can get to the Powell Valley area, I can meet you first thing in the morning. There's a hotel just off Highway 23."

"I'll be there. Drive safe, Doctor."

"You, too, Soren. And it's good to hear from you

again."

Moments after the call ended, Soren's phone died. He tossed it into his suitcase, and as he closed it back up, a voice called to him from below, "Hey! On the roof! What are you doing up there?"

Soren turned to find a policeman had pulled up and was standing beside his car. "Sorry!" Soren shouted back. "I'll be right down!" He got to his feet and got to the edge of the building and bent his knees in preparation.

"Wait—!" the officer gasped, but Soren had already jumped from the roof. Heated light shone from his feet as he bobbed inches above the ground just before landing. "Woah. Did you just…?"

"Yeah, I'm still getting used to it myself," Soren explained with a chuckle.

"Right. Everyone has access to hover gear nowadays, don't they? Drones, maybe?" he tried to convince himself, shaking his head. "You got an ID?"

"Uh… I did. Lost it in an accident a few days ago."

"An accident, huh? Guess I won't pry any further. Just don't make standing on the edge of rooftops too much of a habit. Tends to raise some eyebrows."

"I'll keep that in mind," Soren said. "I should probably get going. Got places to be. Catch you later."

"Oh, and if you're going to fly any more—" the officer advised, a slight chuckle in his voice, but Soren had flown away as he was speaking, "—watch for…planes." He had intended it as a joke about the hovering bit, only to find that the guy could actually fly. Well, rocket was a more accurate description. At mach speeds, at that. Hover gear wouldn't be able to do that. "It's time to retire." The officer returned to his car, where his partner was waiting. As he entered, he was greeted by a barrage of questions.

"Did that man just—?" his partner asked in awe.

"Yep," he replied.

"I wasn't seeing things?"

"Nope."

"And you were face-to-face with him."

"Yep."

"Wild… You kept your cool pretty well."

"Thanks. Is it almost end of shift yet?"

"Nah. Still got almost five hours."

"Oh. How should we put this in the report?"

"You're the one in charge. I should be asking you."

"How about we just pretend nothing happened?"

"Roger, that."

"Since we're here, would you care for a donut?"

"Sounds good to me."

CHAPTER 03
THE STAR BUSTER

Mark Twain National Forest, Missouri
Sunday, August 01, 2027

Keeping to a low altitude, Soren was making a leisurely pace over the canopy of trees. He had a lot of time left in the day to cover a distance that could be made in little more than a handful of hours with a car. In the air, he could easily cut the travel time in half.

It was quiet as the sea of green passed him underneath. He passed too quickly for the chirping of the birds to reach his ears in full. The happenings of the forest were in fast-forward. Far to his left and many meters above an airplane passed, the only sound that lasted more than a moment.

But strangely, even after it passed, the sound of an engine did not fade. As he looked around, he saw nothing abnormal. Nothing above him, behind him, below him. Nothing on his flanks. Yet *something* was making that noise.

And then it hit him—literally.

Soren was sent freewheeling through the air, his suitcase falling out of his hand as he barely managed to generate enough energy to stay airborne before he crashed into the trees. He turned to face whatever it was that had struck him, and was stunned to see an eight-foot-tall azure humanoid machine floating toward him.

"Test Subject Quasar, surrender now! You are wanted for the destruction of government property and evading arrest," a familiar voice demanded from within the machine.

"Harold? The guy from the bunker, right? I was wondering when you might catch up," Soren taunted, but he watched carefully around him to be sure the officer hadn't brought backup. One punch from one of these machines was already more than enough for Soren's day.

"I told you, it's Command Sergeant Major to you."

"That's too long, sorry. I'll stick to calling you Harold," Soren said, floating higher into the air. Though he tried to sound braver than he felt, he used his height as a means to discreetly survey his surroundings further.

"I'll warn you once, Doctor: move much more and I'll have to resort to force," Bolton commanded, flying the mech to a higher altitude than his quarry.

"Bit late for that, Harold," Soren egged on, taking the high ground once again, picking up speed as they both ascended. At this point, Soren was confident Bolton had brought no reinforcements, and a slight wave of relief washed over him. All the same, he remained wary of the great machine that hovered before him, an armor that encased the man that Soren was sure would become a repeated thorn in his side.

Two large cannons sprouted from the shoulders of the machine. "Remember, you chose this," Bolton warned before launching two bursts of plasma from the cannons in Soren's direction.

Soren narrowly avoided the attacks as he dived toward the ground. "Who knew our government had equipment like this, huh?" he asked as he flared his own viridian energy toward the body of the machine. Yet it roared against a near-invisible forcefield that kept Bolton safe from harm. "Even has fancy sci-fi shields like you see in the movies. Any other tricks that Transformer of yours has up its sprockets?" He had to keep the fear out of his voice. Maybe if he kept Bolton talking he could figure a way out of this. He apparently wasn't faster than it, based on how quickly he had been overtaken, but he was a smaller target by more than two and a half feet.

"Impressed? This suit is designed to destroy nuclear weapons and survive the explosion, radiation, and all. It's called... the Star Buster." The machine swooped toward Soren. One large hand grasped him around the middle and had begun to force him toward the ground.

Soren fired at the head of the machine time and time again, but just as he thought the shielding was beginning to flicker, the two smashed into the trees, crashing through branches and leaves for only a moment before they struck the soil.

The doctor tumbled backward, only coming to a halt when his back hit a tree trunk and he slumped to the forest floor. The machine stood up as the dust cloud cleared. "Well, Doctor," Bolton asked, "had enough?"

Soren felt blood pooling in his mouth from having bit his own tongue during the fall; he spat a glob of the crimson fluids to the ground at Bolton's feet. "Sorry to rob you of the satisfaction, but now it's my turn," he retorted. Soren rocketed toward the center of the mech suit, discharging energy just like when he had escaped from the bunker, but this time, he made sure to use plenty of electromagnetism. If he was to have any chance of beating that shield, his best bet was to short it out.

Once again, the two were airborne as Soren pushed back against Bolton's machine. Soren's blasts again caused the shields to flicker, and with another moment of firing energy into them, they disappeared. Yet when the energy hit the suit, it barely seemed affected by the heat. "Thanks," Bolton said sarcastically. "It was starting to get a bit cold in here." The mech then swung one oversized arm and batted Soren away. Again, the doctor tumbled into the forest. "I hate to have to do this. I had really hoped we could get along when I first found you."

Once Soren had smashed to the ground, leaving a trail of smoldering brush in his path, Bolton unleashed two more explosions of plasma in his direction. Soren only just managed to generate enough energy to rocket out of the way, using the bright flash of light from the Star Buster's own projectiles as cover.

When the smoke cleared, there was nothing but a pair of smoldering craters where the doctor had been only a moment ago. Bolton flicked on the heat sensors built into his suit, but they malfunctioned. Unable to pick up any sign as to the doctor's demise, Bolton cursed. "Dammit. He pushed this thing further than we expected."

The giant machine flew away, and Soren waited a few moments, trying to recuperate. Still lying on the ground, he felt something heave in his stomach. He had just enough time to roll over and get his hands and knees beneath him before his breakfast came back up, leaving the forest floor painted with regurgitated icing.

"Guess I ate a bit much to be fighting like that," he muttered to himself, and he noticed a squirrel eyeing him cautiously. "What, you think I look funny?" he said, and the rodent only tilted its head. "Fine, whatever," Soren resolved.

"I can't go to a hospital. They'll just find me again," he considered. "I need to get something to fix these wounds up with, though." As he attempted to get his feet beneath him, intense pain shot up from the left side of his back and his left ankle. "Shit!" he yelled as he doubled over again.

He took careful breaths as he attempted to gather his thoughts. "Doesn't feel like I've broken anything," he thought, forcing his brain through a self-diagnosis. "Just a sprain in the foot and a pulled muscle in the back. Hurts like hell, though." He looked around at his surroundings again, and noticed his suitcase had landed only a couple dozen yards away, and with as much damage as had been done to the forest, there were plenty of fallen tree limbs.

"If I can get some good branches, I can make a splint and have a makeshift crutch as well. Just need a piece of clothing to hold the splint in place," he reasoned. So as pain seared through him, he crawled to the clearing and obtained the bits of brush he needed, carefully fashioning his crutch first from a larger limb. Then, with its help, he was able to limp to his suitcase.

It wasn't the most sturdy or effective, but he pieced together a sort of brace using tube socks and small branches. And at least it did something to dull the pain of using his left leg. Flying was out of the question. He couldn't hold himself straight, so his trajectory would be off by quite a margin.

With his major causes of pain mostly taken care of, he hooked his suitcase over his crutch and began the hike, using the sun to determine the direction he needed to go. Luckily, as he traveled, he managed to come across a highway. He limped along for what felt like over an hour before he saw a single vehicle: an eighteen-wheeler with a covered load.

Hailing the truck with a hitchhiker's thumb, he was amazed when the driver actually brought it to a stop and rolled down the window. "Hey, do you need an ambulance?" the driver called.

"I'm not hurt that badly," Soren replied. "But I could use a ride if you don't mind."

"Sure thing," the man obliged. He looked for a moment like he wanted to ask more about Soren's injuries, but a look from Soren that implied he didn't want to talk about it seemed enough to change the driver's mind. "Where to?" he settled on asking as Soren struggled to pull himself in.

"Depends, how far east can you go?" Soren countered, hissing from the pain in his left side.

"East? I can go as far as St. Louis, I think."

"It's a deal," Soren agreed, handing the man a one-hundred-dollar bill he had successfully fished from his suitcase.

"Wow. Thanks, man!" the driver exclaimed.

"I'm the one who should be doing the thanking," Soren said, leaning against the window. It wasn't perfectly comfortable, but it was definitely better than trying to walk.

The trucker put the vehicle in drive and began the commute. "Why don't you try to rest a bit?" he suggested. "It'll be a few hours before we get to where we're going. And it looks like you could use it."

"That doesn't sound too bad," Soren conceded. He let himself relax, and within minutes, he was asleep.

"Hey. Hey, guy. Wake up," a voice said, rousing Soren from his sleep.

"Whaddizzit?" Soren muttered, incoherent as his eyes began to open.

"We made it to St. Louis. I figured I'd drop you at a hotel up here. Least I could do with what you tipped," the driver explained.

"Oh, thanks," Soren replied, still trying to blink away the sleep from his eyes.

"Don't mention it," the driver said, shaking Soren's hand. "I suppose this is where we part ways."

"Suppose so," Soren answered. "Stay safe."

"You too, and I hope you get better," the driver wished as Soren climbed out of the truck.

He booked two nights at the hotel, and once he had settled into his room—which was thankfully on the first floor—he used the room's phone to call Doctor Holst again. Soren explained that he ran into trouble, and that he was stuck in St. Louis for the time. Luckily, the old man agreed to drive all the way there, so Soren was free to relax for a day.

And relax he did. The only thing he did during the day he spent waiting was walk to nearby restaurants for food, and there were many within just a few short blocks of the hotel. He would have liked to have studied his condition, but without equipment, he would have to wait on Doctor Holst. So he merely recuperated and watched the news.

"A Washington home seems to have been decimated in another wave of meteor showers that have been stunning residents in the Pacific Northwest for nearly a week now," the news anchor explained as images of the destruction flashed across the screen. "Rescue teams are currently clearing debris in attempts to find the owner of the home, Charles 'Chip' Allen. Allen was reported by friends and family to have been home only minutes before the impact was reported by Allen's neighbors."

The screen changed to show an elderly woman being interviewed on the subject, "I heard a big crash and looked out the window to see Chip's house on fire down the street, so I run to the phone to dial 9-1-1. I didn't realize his house got hit by a asteroid. Oh, I hope they find him okay; he was such a nice boy, Chip—"

The screen cut back to the news anchor. "This is the second such incident that has been reported in the week since the meteor showers began. Earlier this week, astrophysicist Soren Grant was killed in a similar meteor impact." The screen briefly showed a picture of Soren that he recognized as his lab identification, as well as an image of his house that must have been taken between the impact and his visit back home. "We'll bring you more as these stories develop."

To Soren, who remembered the pain from the impact, didn't see the likelihood of his survival if a house had collapsed on him. He felt grimly that Charles would probably be found in pieces, if they found anything at all. Charles had, according to what was implied, suffered a much more direct hit than he had.

It seemed Soren had been incredibly lucky. Or maybe unlucky, depending on how one viewed the situation. On one hand, he would like to find a way to do away with these powers. It was freakish, the things he could do. Normal life would be preferable again. But on the other hand, he was able to do things unlike anything he had done before. He wasn't unlike the superheroes he had seen on TV as a kid.

As a young child, he had imagined himself one day becoming a hero. After all, how many young boys dream of being a superhero, blurring the lines between fantasy and reality? It was natural at that time to believe nearly any myth that passed over his plate—just like Santa Claus or the Easter Bunny.

But as with most things from his youth, he had long since outgrown those delusions. Superheroes weren't any more real than Santa Claus, and that was just something you tell kids to get them excited for the holidays, right? Yet here he was, with powers akin to those you'd find in a comic book, and not a chance in the world of explaining how or why. He laughed at the concept of lumping himself together with Father Christmas, as suddenly, such legends were seeming less far-fetched.

Soren looked himself over in the mirror; he was thin, borderline underweight. His green eyes were faded and ghastly, with small veins of gold piercing through the paled jade ever since the incident. His average brown hair was short, unkempt, and hardly a notable feature. Sure, his adrenaline combined with his powers had helped him to accomplish things he shouldn't be capable of during the fight with the machine, but he was on the run from the government, not fighting crime on the streets like the heroes he remembered. Even if he tried, he was hardly the hero type. He preferred the security of a lab to rushing into danger where thugs—or worse, Bolton with that science-fiction robotic suit of his—would be trying to kill him.

He was a freak, trying to survive when he should have died. So why was he still here? Why did he make it through the meteor? Why, and how, had he gotten powers from it? Science as he knew it could never align with what he had been through, could it? If he ever got Bolton off his back, could he ever return to normal life?

Perhaps he could figure things out with Doctor Holst tomorrow. He shut the television off—no good was coming from it anyway—and rolled into bed, falling into a fitful sleep as dreams of grandeur and nightmares of torment intermingled to create a menagerie of unrest.

CHAPTER 04
ROAD TRIP

St. Louis, Missouri
Tuesday, August 03, 2027

After a night of nearly no sleep, Soren awoke early. According to the clock in his room, it was still only 5:18. Despite being fully alert, he laid in bed staring at the ceiling for another twenty minutes before finally deciding to get up.

In hopes of finding a bit of energy in the feeling of water splashing his face, Soren made for the shower. Aside from a couple of large bruises—one between his shoulders, the other on his right hip—he realized his injuries felt quite significantly better. He flexed his sore joints under the spray of the shower, which did wonders to reinvigorate him. He took his time preparing. Holst was supposed to ring his hotel room when he arrived, which likely wouldn't be until close to checkout time.

For food, he settled simply for the hotel's

complementary breakfast. It wasn't as enjoyable as the donuts he had had in Springfield, but it would suffice. It was 8:31 when he finished eating, and only moments later, the phone rang in the room. Soren didn't need to answer—it only rang twice anyway. Though it was early, he still knew what its purpose was. Looking onto the parking lot from his window, he saw an old van with a familiar face accompanying it.

It took Soren only a minute longer to turn in his room key and stride outside onto the asphalt. Soren waved at his newly arrived and seemingly anxious companion. And as Soren drew closer, the doctor's impatience became more pronounced.

"You've kept me waiting long enough on a story. How did you manage to survive?" Doctor Holst asked, gesturing Soren toward the passenger side door of the 1988 Chevrolet Astro.

"Long story. Believe me, it'll make for a great tale while we're on the road," Soren said, climbing nervously into the passenger seat as Holst took the wheel. "First, are you sure that this old thing can stand up to driving around? It's older than I am," Soren responded, being cautious with any part of the vehicle he touched.

"She's been through a lot, but she's gotten me this far and doesn't show any signs of slowing down," the elder man boasted.

"Alright," Soren warily accepted. The engine roared to life as Holst turned the key in the ignition. The vehicle lurched forward, and Soren was somehow not reassured that it would hold as well as Holst was boasting. But when the elder doctor shot him a glance as if he were expecting the story he had been promised, Soren continued, "So, I'm not sure I can explain the how for certain, but I've become radioactive since the incident."

"Radioactive?!"

"Relax, Doctor," Soren coaxed. "I can control it. Besides, even if I was letting the radiation loose, it's not unlike natural sunlight. As long as I'm not forcing it out at a hundred percent, worst I'd do is give you is a tan, maybe a sunburn."

Holst seemed unconvinced as to his safety as they reached the road, but made no attempt to disengage Soren from the vehicle. "Interesting…" he mused. "I've never heard of anything radioactive having control over the discharge of radiation. I admit, I'm skeptical, but as you did survive a meteor impact, I'll play along."

"I understand your wariness, Doctor," Soren agreed. "Science as I've always understood it doesn't seem to explain what has happened to me. Surely you understand why I would bring such a conundrum to your attention."

When Holst's only response was a shrug and a grunt, Soren continued. "I was held in government custody for a short time, but I did manage to escape. As crazy as this is about to sound, releasing enough energy seems to allow me to... fly."

Holst raised an eyebrow and looked sideways at his passenger. "You're sounding more and more far-fetched, my friend. And I've heard and seen some bizarre things in the field—"

"I know, I know. But you're the only person I can turn to, Doctor," Soren said. "If we weren't in such a closed space right now, I'd demonstrate properly, but as it were..."

Soren focused the radiation to his left index finger, holding it up where his companion could easily see the gleam of heat forming around it, accompanied by a faint green light.

"Holy—!" Hardwin exclaimed, nearly swerving off the road. "Okay, so you're hot. And if the rest of your story is to be believed, on the run from the government?"

"Yep," Soren said, almost matter-of-factly as if this were something normal. Of course, to him, it was slowly becoming the norm.

"I have to say this was not what I was expecting to hear today, my friend."

"It's not what I was expecting to be relaying to you when I said I'd be coming to visit," Soren grimaced.

Holst pondered for a minute. "So our best bet..." he wondered aloud, "is probably to live on the road for a bit. Keep ourselves secluded."

"I'd agree, but I need to know: do you have a lab we can use to study?" Soren asked, pulling the canister containing the meteorite fragment from his suitcase to display. "I have a lot about my condition and this sample that I still need to learn."

"Do I have—Soren, who do you think you're talking to?" Doctor Holst blurted. "Just look behind you!"

Soren turned in his seat and saw an impressive fold-up laboratory full of equipment. A telescope, a computer, and a centrifuge were barely scratching the surface of all the gadgets he saw. Soren would have never expected to see them all fit together in the back of a van. "Amazing," he noted.

"Wait until you see it expanded," the doctor boasted. "So where to first?"

"Not sure. Somewhere remote. Far enough from either of our homes, but not too obvious a choice. Nowhere with anyone we know."

"Somewhere like Ellison Bay, Wisconsin?" Hardwin offered.

"I don't even know where that is," Soren chuckled.

"I've only been in its vicinity once in my life. Kept it in mind in case I needed to get away."

"You mean you expected to have to be on the run like this?" Soren retorted.

"Oh, nothing as dramatic as our current predicament, but if the lab ever came knocking with some project or another, it's nice to be able to get away from them. I know I said some research would be welcome, but, well, there are some projects I've been involved in over the years that an old fellow would like to not repeat."

"Now you've got me worried I could be one of those," Soren said with a laugh.

"Hmmm… Might be. Might have to leave you somewhere and go on my own."

"You weren't supposed to agree!"

"Only joking, only joking," Holst said, stifling a guffaw of his own. "How about some tunes? It'll be a long drive as it is, might as well give ourselves some kind of entertainment."

"Have at it," Soren replied, and Holst kicked on a 1900s rock station, proving just how old fashioned he was.

Holst explained as they drove that the plan would be to avoid any toll roads; getting on one of them would potentially subject them to government scrutiny. And they weren't going to be able to use the lab until their trip was finished. Their use of it even then would have to be discreet, otherwise someone might misunderstand the intents of the lab and report them to the authorities.

Even without such a mix-up, their possession of radioactive material could definitely raise some alarms. Only select people were supposed to have access to meteor fragments from the recent showers, and Soren had effectively lost those privileges when he was pronounced "dead".

When they reached this point, Holst told Soren, "By the way, I brought something so that people won't be gawking at you over the fact that you're supposed to have died, especially considering the news stories are becoming more detailed and more widespread. Open the glove compartment."

Soren did as he was told, and had to resist the urge to laugh at what he found. "A ball cap and sunglasses. You're kidding, right?"

"Old school though it may be," Holst explained, "it's effective enough for people to not immediately recognize who you are."

"If you say so."

The rest of the day's driving was spent with Holst asking for details about what had happened to Soren since the meteor. Soren told him more about the bunker and his escape, his return home to find it decimated, and his encounter with Bolton between Springfield and St. Louis, which the doctor took particular interest in. But it seemed that no matter how much detail he gave, he couldn't sate Holst's craving for information. Soren wondered whether they would actually make it all the way to Wisconsin before opening the lab, and why the doctor was playing music if he only insisted on conversing over it anyway.

Holst's route took them through Effingham and Champaign to get to Chicago for their first day of driving. Normally this would have taken much less time to drive, but Holst, in his old age, needed frequent breaks, and the antiquated vehicle wasn't capable of going as fast as a more modern car would have been. As a result, the drive just to Chicago took until after seven that evening.

By that time, Soren was thankful that he was so exhausted, because he fell right to sleep while Holst continued to ask questions from the other bed. Not that he had much more to tell. Holst's questions had at this point exceeded Soren's own knowledge about his condition.

Soren awoke the next morning feeling better

rested than he had in a long time. After he and Holst had their breakfasts, the doctor insisted on a more practical demonstration of Soren's powers. Soren agreed, so they found a secluded road outside of the city—and quite outside of their intended route—where Soren wouldn't be seen by the populace.

Of course, the performance Soren was about to give off was not only for the doctor's satisfaction. Soren himself was curious about what he could do when he wasn't in a life-or-death situation. Thus, he began to float off the ground slowly, and Holst was elated.

"Brilliant! This is incredible!" he shouted.

Soren smirked. Holst had seen nothing yet.

And so Soren launched himself skyward, performing figure-eights and loop-de-loops, flips and barrel rolls. Once, he shot into a dive, pulling up only inches from the ground and rocketed off again. When he looked back, he saw a burning patch of grass where he had come so close to hitting the earth, and he couldn't help but smile. Before he returned to the doctor's side, he decided to try one last thing for the day. He flew toward a lone tree adjacent to the field they were in, and built up energy in his right hand until he held what seemed to be an orb of brilliant emerald flame the size of a tennis ball. Then he threw the fireball at the trunk of the tree with all his might.

Soren hadn't tried proper long-range attacks with his powers yet, and wasn't sure what to expect out of it. But to his amazement—and to Doctor Hardwin's as well by the sound of his reaction—the sphere flashed toward the tree with the speed of a bullet. It struck the trunk dead center and burst; wood chips and embers soared from the epicenter of the explosion, and the top half of the tree toppled to the ground. The now exposed and splintered inner layers of the tree smoldered as Soren passed over it.

When Soren returned to the doctor, the latter's eyes were wide. "That… that was…" But what it was, Soren never got to hear, as Holst had fallen silent momentarily for loss of words.

Soren himself was a bit short of breath. He had exerted a lot of energy for the demonstration. The only time he had used that much energy for his power, he had nearly faced death at the hands of

Bolton's machine. "Satisfied?" he panted out.

"Oh, absolutely," Holst sang. "Soren, you're a superhuman! I've seen a lot of scientific advancements in my day, but... well, this takes the cake."

Soren felt a small pang of regret suddenly. "Doctor, with all due respect, I would hardly call this a scientific advancement. I should be dead due to what resulted in this, and believe me, I wouldn't recommend standing under a falling meteor to anyone who would want powers like this."

Holst's face became stern again. "Sorry, Soren, I meant no ill by it. But you can't deny, the fact that you can do something like this—well, it's kind of incredible, isn't it?" Holst cautiously patted Soren on the back, as if afraid he might get burned.

"But will it be worth it in the end?" Soren asked. "Don't get me wrong, I'd love to use this power for the good of everyone—it's the right thing to do, after all, isn't it? But I'm worried I'll never be able to if I have to keep running from the government my whole life. I mean, who knows how many more of those robot suits they may have in store?"

"Soren, you're one of the brightest students I've ever had the pleasure of teaching, but powers like this are a bit out of my league. I can't tell you how to use them or how to do things right by them, or even how to get the government off your back. But one thing I can tell you is that you've always had a good heart, and I know you'll do your best to do right, no matter what challenges face you." His expression softened again, and when he spoke, his tone had become brighter once more. "Now, what say you to getting back on the road? We've got a lot of ground to cover."

Soren nodded. He didn't trust himself to speak at the moment. Doctor Holst had said it: Soren could—and would—find a way to do things the right way. He would use this power to help people in need of it. It didn't matter if Bolton chased him to the ends of the earth.

And so they took their seats in the van once again, Holst putting on his old rock music once more as they rumbled back onto the interstate. The day as a whole was relatively quieter than the day before. Holst seemed to have decided that further questions would get him nowhere further than the demonstration from earlier that day, and Soren was lost in his own thoughts anyway.

The route this time started with a number of smaller roads that were rather boring stretches of land with little to look at. They passed through a couple of small towns before they reached Milwaukee around midday. There, they stopped for gas before they would resume their venture to Ellison Bay.

As they pulled up to a pump, Holst handed Soren a small handful of cash. "Would you mind running in to pay for me? Don't forget your disguise," he said with a grin.

Soren agreed, and after donning the cap and shades, strode leisurely to the building. Inside, he handed the doctor's money to the cashier, indicating which pump he was on. After getting the receipt, he turned around only to find his nose in the barrel of a handgun.

His assailant was masked, wearing a denim jacket and gloves, and demanded the cashier and Soren turn over any money they had. Soren, however, did not move right away, and he remembered Holst's words from earlier that day:

"You've always had a good heart, and I know you'll do your best to do right, no matter what challenges face you."

"Hey, loser, the cashier has the harder job, and she's gonna be done before you at this rate. Put your money in the bag!" the crook demanded, but Soren simply focused on the gun an inch from his face. He could feel the heat emanating from himself, and knew his face had begun to glow.

"What the hell are—OW!" the bandit yelled, dropping the gun. It had quickly become hot in his hand from Soren's energy output, and the cashier stopped loading the money bag for a moment. "No one said you could stop! Just because this guy's a frea—" But he never finished his sentence, as Soren had struck him in the gut with a glowing fist. The burglar doubled over and dropped his bag as well.

Soren wasn't sure what he was doing. He let his body act on its own. And next thing he knew, he had grabbed the criminal by the front of his jacket and launched himself with the robber out the front doors. As Soren let go, the burglar tumbled onto the asphalt, and two other men had begun to approach the scene. Soren addressed one of them.

"This man was trying to rob the store. Hold him here until the police arrive if you can. I should probably go..." he said, realizing that they were gawking at him, and he understood why. Aside from him having just literally flown out of a building, he had lost his hat and glasses in the brief moments of action. Aside from a robbery in the middle of the day, they were staring at a supposedly dead person who was capable of flight.

And indeed his suspicions as to their thoughts were confirmed in the next moment as one of them spoke up. "Wait, aren't you that guy from the news? The one who's supposed to be dead?"

But by the time he had finished, Soren had flown away. He landed atop a nearby building where he could lay low enough as to not be seen, but where he could still keep an eye out for the doctor and when he might leave. The police arrived before that happened, though, and apprehended the thief with ease.

Shortly after the arrival of the police, Soren

saw Holst's van leave the parking lot, and he flew after it overhead. The glow he gave off would be barely noticeable against the midday sun. He was careful to keep an eye on the old van until it pulled in behind a local restaurant.

Soren dropped to the ground as Holst removed himself from the van. "Soren!" the doctor proclaimed as he saw his younger friend. "That was incredible! I'm glad you managed to follow me. I was a bit worried about where you might have gone to after the excitement."

"I'd have been much worse off without you, Doctor," Soren reassured him. "But I needed to make sure the police didn't see me when they showed up."

"Ah, right, right," the elder man replied. "Well, that was a right brilliant thing you did back there, stopping a robbery like that."

"Thanks," Soren grimaced.

"I knew you'd find a way to put your powers to good use, and look at you now! A proper superhero!"

"Wait, a—a what?!" Soren exclaimed. He had to have heard him incorrectly.

"A superhero! Everyone at the station was talking about it after you disappeared. The two people who kept watch over the crook, the cashier, a couple others, and they all told the police that it was a flying superhero who had taken down the perp. Thankfully, the cashier didn't tell them I was with you, or I could have been in for some questioning about this flying person business—"

"Doctor, there's some kind of mistake. I'm not a superhero. Someone was doing wrong and I had the ability to do something about—"

"No, no. No mistake about it. You saved someone's life and put a stop to a villain. And you can fly and do your glowing stuff and everything. Sounds plenty superhero-like to me!"

Soren was dumbfounded. He didn't feel like a hero. But now a number of people were reportedly calling him one. Like one of the guys from the comics. Maybe he could tell the doctor the one detail he had left out during all his explaining the day before.

"Doctor," he said in a low voice.

"What's the matter?"

What was he thinking? He had used the alias once before because he was supposed to be dead. It wouldn't have done to use his real name. There was no sense—none—in telling Holst about the alias Bolton had given him. He wasn't a superhero, even if he had had moments that he felt like one. He was just a person who had been bestowed some supernatural powers, right? It could have been anyone.

"Never mind," he said after a moment of consideration. "Let's just get back on the road, if we can."

The doctor agreed, and they drove on again, now slightly delayed but still on schedule to reach Ellison Bay that night, even if they drove a little later than the previous day. The remainder of the trip was spent with Holst gushing about Soren's heroics, and Soren wishing he would stop. Normally, Soren would have been ecstatic to be receiving praise of this magnitude, especially from his mentor. But this time, he was less enthusiastic.

He wasn't sure why, either. When it came to these powers, he had thus far been contempt with talking down to that self-important sergeant Bolton. In fact, he was still more than ready to put Bolton in his place, and he'd do it with a smile. Maybe it was the weight—the reality—of his situation that was catching up to him. Maybe it was the fact that he knew he had further responsibility now, that there would be an expectation to do good with this power. Regardless, he was now feeling overwhelmed, and he hoped that the research in the coming days would help set his mind straight.

As expected, they reached Ellison Bay late that night. They were able to find an abandoned farm just outside the town, and it was there that they set up what would be their new research base for a few days. Holst provided sleeping bags, which they put to use in the creaky, moonlit loft of an old barn.

CHAPTER 05
THE LAB IN THE VAN

Ellison Bay, Wisconsin
Thursday, August 05, 2027

Soren had helped expand the van-lab and Holst was now hooking up the solar power generator to all the different machines. He had been right: the lab was even more impressive after expansion. It shouldn't have logically been able to cram into the back of a vehicle of such size. Yet here it was, blowing away Soren's expectations. Apparently Doctor Holst had taken extreme care in putting everything together in order to waste as little space as possible.

Holst finished plugging everything in, and monitors flashed to life, lights began blinking, and it seemed all would be in working order. Soren was quickly filled with excitement at the prospect of working at such a station with his old mentor. He took a seat, but Holst quickly stopped him.

"I know you're urgent for answers," Holst

began, "but in order to get them, we're going to have to run tests on you first."

Soren's heart sank. Alas, he was going to have to be tested on before he could do any testing of his own. "Over here," Holst said, directing Soren to a different chair near the centrifuge. "I'm going to have to take some blood samples for our first batch of tests. Don't worry, my hands are still plenty steady to do this," he continued, noticing the look of concern on Soren's face.

"Alright," Soren consented, leaning back in the chair and presenting his left arm in preparation for the needle that would soon be inserted. And indeed Holst was more steady of hand than Soren expected. The blood drawing took only a minute before Holst was finished.

The blood was placed in the centrifuge, and Holst ushered Soren back to the computers. "Where's that sample of space rock you had before?" he asked Soren. Soren retrieved it from his bag, and Holst placed it in another machine. As the centrifuge spun, it seemed to have already begun transmitting certain data to the computer. At the same time, the computer seemed to be collecting data from the meteor sample, and was displaying charts including the data from each sample.

While Soren had been expecting certain similarities to the rock's radioactivity within his own blood stream, he didn't expect the properties to be quite so similar. In fact, the two charts that the computer was generating were only just shy of identical. "Incredible," Holst muttered as he clicked through even more charts and data that had been generated. Soren took his own seat and began searching through the data. He was at a loss for words.

It took the computer an hour to finish compiling all the data from the tests it seemed to be running in sync. Never once did the collected information differ between the samples any more than an infinitesimal amount. "Doctor," Soren finally said. "Have you ever seen anything like this?"

The doctor stared at the screen a moment longer with his mouth hanging slightly ajar. Then at last he responded, "Never. Not the rock, not a person so… in tune with radiation like this. Your DNA seems to have reacted almost perfectly with this meteor."

"No kidding," Soren said, returning his own gaze to the charts displayed before him.

"I'm going to have to run some more tests—check the samples every couple hours. I want to see what kind of half-life this stuff has."

Soren shook himself. For whatever reason he hadn't considered that he might have a half-life on his powers as well. "Let me know when you run those tests again. I'd like to see what's happening."

"Oh, you didn't think we were done gathering information out of you, did you?" Holst asked, raising an eyebrow. "Give me a strand of your hair. Just one will do."

"Wha—?" Soren went to ask, but Holst had already reached to yank a single hair from Soren's scalp. He attached each end to a separate clip, flipped a couple of switches, and the computer began gathering data on it as well, though different statistics from before. It seemed to be measuring the conductivity of the thin strand, which, to Soren's amazement once again, seemed to be significantly more conductive than a normal human hair.

"That'll be the electromagnetism you told me about," said Holst, though more to the air than to Soren in particular. "Now let's test heat."

Holst flipped two more switches and began fidgeting with a dial, and the hair began to glow hot. Holst adjusted the temperature both up and down, and at no point did the hair show signs of becoming more brittle because of it. Eventually, he decided to turn the heat all the way up. The strand of hair glowed white, but still showed no sign of combusting or breaking apart.

The remainder of the day passed with further such tests awing the two scientists, and as the sun began to set, Holst had finally reached a conclusion pertaining to the mineral's half-life. "It seems it diminishes very slowly. Levels have only changed exceptionally minutely since we've begun the trial. If the pattern continues, the half-life would be roughly five hundred years, if I'm not mistaken."

"Five hundred!" Soren exclaimed. "So my powers likely won't see any major depreciation over the span of my life?

"Likely not," Holst continued. "However, you told

me that you had, in a sense, died prior to these powers awakening and your return to life, correct?"

"Yes, but what does that have to do with anything?"

"I have a theory, and do keep in mind that that is all it is. But I believe, based on this information, that your life force and your powers may be connected. There is a chance that your heart may continue to beat as long as the powers are strong enough to keep it going."

Soren looked stunned. "You mean there's a chance of me living a much longer life?"

"Again, it is only a theory, but there is a chance. While I would love to find proof of it, and while I have an expanse of equipment here, the exact equipment that would be needed to prove it is not here. To make matters worse, to my knowledge, we wouldn't even be able to perform an MRI or X-Ray or anything of the sort on you without your powers potentially interfering with the machines. So, until we find a way to look inside you without your magnetism disrupting the process, we can only speculate."

"I—I don't know what to make of this. I mean, a long life is great and all, but say I live a few hundred years. That's a long time to have the 'superhero' expectation you were talking about on my shoulders, especially considering it's not exactly a path I want to walk at present," Soren said, his brow furrowed in thought.

"It would be, but then, it might work out for the best, you never know."

"Easy for you to say. You're not the one with the powers."

Holst shrugged and returned to the data to see if there was anything there worth seeing that he hadn't already gone over. "I have a theory on how to make the most of those powers, though. A way to keep you from burning your clothes if you have need of using more than just your exposed skin for channeling them."

"Another theory?"

"Well, I'd go into detail, but I want to test it. I'll let you know when I've got something more solid. For now, let's take it easy. We've been studying too long. I'm ready for a break."

"I'll second that," Soren agreed.

As they reclined, Holst looked sideways at Soren. "D'you have an alias, yet?"

"A what?" Soren asked, puzzled.

"An alias, you know? Alter ego? Hero name?"

Soren sighed. Of course it was only a matter of time before he was asked this question. "Kind of. It's not one I made up myself, but Bolton's crew apparently titled me 'Test Subject Quasar'. So 'Quasar' is the best I've got for you."

"Quasar..." Holst muttered, as if turning it over in his mind. "Not bad. I like it."

Soren wasn't sure what Holst was planning, but without the elder scientist giving him any information, he walked out into the field and looked up at the stars. It seemed like he might be expected to uphold the ideals of being a hero. He tried to talk himself into it. He wasn't opposed to the flashy parts, and he had handled himself well in multiple life-threatening situations already.

He decided to clear his head a bit, and rocketed into the sky. People would already be talking of the flying man who had done extraordinary things. From the man he had encountered in Nevada, to the military troops who were stationed at the wreckage of his home, to the policeman he spoke to in Springfield, and the people he had saved from a gunman in Milwaukee, they all knew about him. He was too well known to be able to disappear now. And he had even done a good deed expected from a vigilante superhuman.

That raised more concerns. What if Bolton was able to follow the trail? Would he be able to figure out that Soren was in Wisconsin? Or would he believe him to have flown even further north, or perhaps turned one direction or another? Suddenly, Soren didn't want to be sitting still. Though he hadn't drawn any attention to himself in Ellison Bay as of yet, Bolton may be scouring the state as he and Holst were doing research.

It was then that Soren realized, if patterns continued, he would likely be running from Bolton for at least the remainder of Bolton's life, if not his own. And eventually, Bolton might catch up to him again. Last time hadn't gone so well, and it was likely to repeat again, or even go worse, if Soren's only course of action was to run.

Thus, he made his decision. While Holst was working on research, Soren would have to practice honing his abilities. It was a bit late to start training in martial arts, but when one can fly and create fireballs, it tends to give an edge anyway.

Over the next days, Soren began a rigorous training regimen, not just testing how far he could push his abilities, but physically training his body. While the progress was not swift by any means, he was noticing some improvement.

Then, roughly two weeks after their arrival, Holst approached Soren during his training. "Soren, I think I've finished my project. If you don't mind following me to the silo, I'd like to show you what it is."

"Sure," Soren agreed. "But can you really not tell me what it is?"

"Oh, no, definitely not," said Holst enigmatically. "If I told you, it'd spoil the surprise."

So Soren followed in silence as Holst opened the door of the abandoned silo. "No," Soren cringed in embarrassment.

"But of course," Holst said, a grin on his wrinkled face. "If you're going to be a superhero, you need to look the part."

In front of Soren, enveloping a mannequin that Holst had procured from who-knows-where was a suit that looked like something from out of a comic book. A midnight blue body glove was partly encased in silvery white armor. Golden accents adorned the joints, and emblazoned on the chest, directly in the center was a golden shape that looked akin to the spiral of a galaxy with a slash from its center beyond its lower right, giving it a vague similarity to the letter "Q".

"It took a bit to get the metallic composition just right, include the right weaves and the like, but the meteor sample you brought along seemed to have slowed its half-life to nearly double its previous duration while encased in this exact type of build," Holst explained. "Speaking of which, I've elected to dub that mineral quasinium, if it's all the same to you."

"Sure," replied Soren, only half taking in the doctor's words. He had taken to striding around the suit, looking at it from all angles.

"I'll leave you for a bit, and I want you to try it on," Holst said, exiting the silo and closing the door behind him.

Soren figured out the various clasps of the armor, which would be easier to reach from the front than expected. He removed his outer layers of clothing and donned the body glove first. It was surprisingly comfortable. Then he clasped the armored parts around his feet, joints, and chest. They hindered his movement only slightly, but were overall unobtrusive.

Looking down at himself, he couldn't help but think he looked a little tacky wearing the outfit, but if it helped channel his powers, perhaps it would help him if he ever fought Bolton again.

Then, his urge to be showy again took control. He focused the energy in his feet and hands, and rocketed into the air, shooting for the ceiling of the old silo. With now improved ease, he tossed a fireball ahead of himself and melted a hole in the tin roof only a moment before he shot out into the open air. He dived to Holst's location, slowing and making himself upright only just before meeting the ground.

"So?" Holst asked. "Like it?"

"Not bad," said Soren, a smile crossing his mouth now.

"I hoped you'd like it. Now, I can't help but think we may have stayed in one place too long. Perhaps we should think about moving on again."

Soren chuckled. "I agree on moving, doctor. But not for the same reasons. Let's go back to Chicago."

"Chicago?! I thought you wanted to lie low," Holst voiced, clearly concerned.

"I've realized the only way to get Bolton off my back will be to face him and settle it mono e mono," Soren explained. "Might as well give him some incentive."

"Ah, taking the hero's route at last?" Holst said, flashing his false teeth.

"Didn't seem to be much of an option. The alternative doesn't look fun."

"Shall we hit the road now, then?"

"Hmmm… How about I meet you there?" Soren said, beginning to hover above the ground again.

Holst gave a nod and a mock salute. "Godspeed, Quasar."

And Soren took to the skies again, leaving Ellison Bay behind.

CHAPTER 06
ORSON LABS

Joseph, Oregon
Friday, August 20, 2027

Despite telling Holst that he would be going to Chicago, Soren had decided that there was one more stop he had to make before trying his hand at "playing the hero" there. By the time Holst reached the city, Soren would be back anyway.

He was now flying much faster than before, due in part to the time he had spent honing his powers and also due to his new suit helping to amplify and focus them. He even had a bit of fun during the flight by soaring alongside a commercial plane briefly before rocketing ahead of it with ease. Eventually, he was home again, and entering his former workplace through the visitor's entrance.

Without looking up from her work, the small woman at the desk addressed him. "Name, please?"

"Soren Grant," Soren said. "Nice to see you again, Bea."

Bea finally looked up from her papers, and her jaw fell so wide, Soren wondered for a moment if it had come unhinged. "*Soren?!*" she exclaimed, jumping up from her desk. Within moments she had exited her small windowed office and had rushed around to where Soren was standing and embraced him in a big hug.

"We all heard you were dead! Why didn't you contact us sooner?" she pressed. Then she took a step back and asked him, "And what on earth are you wearing?"

"It's… complicated," he said hesitantly. "Is Doctor Orson in? I'd like to speak with him."

"Sure, sure," Bea said. "Come on into the office and have a seat; I'll call him right up for you."

Thanks," Soren replied, but she was already pulling him along. For someone a foot shorter than he was—and slimmer, too—she was quite strong.

As she sat back at the desk and called the founder to the front, Soren sat and watched her. She was, Soren thought, pretty. Her hair was shoulder-length and auburn, her eyes a bluish-green. Her smile was accented by dimples and a handful of freckles on her cheeks. He had been good friends with her when they worked together, and he had nearly worked up the courage to ask her out before the meteor changed his life. Now, he didn't dare consider it.

The idea of being something as far-fetched as a superhero and trying to ask someone out just seemed absurd in that moment. Then there would also be the concern of him possibly causing sunburns or worse for anyone he tried to join in a relationship with. He didn't fancy the idea of accidentally turning his significant other into homemade barbecue because he got too close.

After she had paged Doctor Orson, she spun her chair around to look at him. "So come on, spill the beans. How'd you survive? And since when do you wear getup like that? We've got time before Orson gets here."

"That's actually part of why I'm here. To put it simply, I'm not entirely certain I can return to normal life."

"Soren, we both know you're not normal," Bea

teased.

Soren shrugged, but allowed himself a chuckle. "It's a little more than that. I promise I'll explain it all properly when Doctor Orson gets up here. He needs to hear it, too."

And in less than a minute, the founder of the laboratory had arrived at the desk. "So where's this visitor, Miss Bea?"

"In here, Doctor," she replied cheerily.

The dark-skinned scientist peered past Bea through the window and saw Soren sitting in a chair. "Long time, no see, eh, boss?" Soren greeted.

"Soren! You're alive! Coming back to work perhaps? Not planning to work dressed as the tin man, I hope?"

"Sadly, no," Soren nervously began. "I'm actually here to ask for a favor."

"Certainly, what do you require?"

"I need you to run some tests," Soren said. When the doctor nodded, he added, "On me."

Orson looked slightly appalled. "Soren, what's happened?" He entered the office and sat in a seat across from his former employee.

So he told them both about how he had been indirectly affected by the meteor's impact; about how its radiation had altered his DNA, giving him powers; about his and Holst's findings and research; about how Holst had designed a suit to better contain and channel Soren's new powers; and about how Holst had theorized that the radiation might be exactly what was keeping Soren alive, and that his life force may be tied to its strength.

Throughout his tale, Bea gasped and cheered at all the appropriate places, being a very engaged listener. Meanwhile, Orson was silent, looking down at his folded hands with an expression that might imply he was trying with all his might to figure out what it was that lay clasped in his lap. As Soren finished his story, and Orson cast him a look of mild disbelief, Soren conjured a burning orb in his hand. Orson's face turned to shock immediately.

They sat another moment in silence before Orson spoke again. "So if I'm understanding you correctly, you're wanting to figure out first if old Holst's theory is true, and if so, how long you'd have to live?"

Soren nodded.

"I can't guarantee our equipment would work. From the sound of things, you'd be generating a lot of interference, but we can try. Just a warning, though: if everything you've told me is true, this isn't going to be a comfortable experience."

"Believe me, I've been through a lot of discomfort since the incident. A little more shouldn't hurt."

Soren followed Orson out of the office and to a lab at the back of the building. He entered a small restroom and changed from Holst's suit into a hospital gown and inserted a pair of earplugs. At Orson's instruction, Soren entered a small chamber that had only enough light within for Soren to see his way onto the cot within. He laid down and prepared for what he knew the machines around him would do.

A sound strong enough to deafen anyone who failed to wear their earplugs correctly bombarded him while he felt magnets pulling him from every direction. Had he been a normal human, the magnets would have had no effect, but his radiation responded strongly and his arms and legs spread out and gave him the appearance of someone trying to make snow angels while having a seizure.

He knew that x-rays would also be trying to get whatever readings they could. Any methods that could get a look at his insides and more were running simultaneously. He felt his stomach almost literally jump against his lower ribs along with his lungs and his heart. He felt like his insides were trying to escape his body, but couldn't find their way out. Breathing became nearly impossible and only came in small spurts. He didn't dare open his mouth for fear of throwing up or worse. Despite wanting to scream from the agony, he managed to keep his sounds to only grunts and groans of pain.

He clenched his eyes shut against the awful feeling. While he knew he was in no real danger, it didn't make things any better. His head was spinning and throbbing all at the same time. He could barely feel the cot beneath him. He was shaking against his will as the sounds continued to reverberate through his every molecule.

Then, after only seconds that felt like an eternity, it ended and Orson opened the door for him. Soren found his way upright with difficulty and bolted for the restroom as quickly as he could, not even sure which way was up or down as he did.

Once his stomach had ceased emptying itself, Soren made his way wearily back to Orson, who was sitting behind a computer while a larger screen opposite him displayed charts and various scans. "Feeling alright?" he asked as Soren sank into a chair beside him.

"I've been better," Soren said, still clutching his abdomen. "What did you find?"

"Well, it's not easy to tell, but I'm sure you felt it. The radiation has worked its way into your very organs. In fact, Holst seems to have been right in theorizing that that is *exactly* why you came back to life. The energy inside you seems to have jump started your heart."

"Yeah, that seems to be hard to deny after that," Soren grimaced.

"With that, we can safely deduce that your vitals will be tied to the half-life of this radiation.

Now, I'll give your heart a chance to settle, and I need to check your pulse. When you feel ready, let me know and we'll walk back to the front. When you can handle that, I'll know you'll be ready for the last bit."

Soren gave a thumbs up and continued to catch his breath. While he did so, Orson continued to study the scans. After another minute or two, the nausea had left him and the aching had partly subsided. Soren spoke up again, "I think I'm ready."

"Excellent. I'll follow you just to be sure you're okay. Oh, and you may want to change back out of that gown."

Soren changed again in the restroom, then they made their way back to the front and rejoined Bea in her office. Soren felt his heart jump again, and it had nothing to do with the scan he had been through. He forced himself to slow his breathing discreetly to ensure his heart rate would be normal when Orson checked it.

They took their former seats across from each other and Orson took Soren's wrist in hand and observed his watch. "How'd it go?" Bea asked.

"Rough," Soren said. "It was like I was a

ragdoll."

Bea giggled. "You're supposed to keep it professional, doctors."

Orson shot her a less-than-entertained glance before returning his gaze to his watch for only a moment longer. "Well, you're on the high side of normal, but nothing that anyone would normally need to be concerned about," he explained as he released Soren's wrist. "Might still be a little high because of the scans. But as long as you remain in normal range, you should still be fine for roughly as long as the half-life of the radiation. Out of curiosity, how long did you say that was again?"

"Five hundred years," Soren muttered.

Bea's eyes went wide. "You mean Soren could live to be five hundred?"

"Maybe more, maybe less," Orson shrugged. "It's a bit of guesswork right now, honestly. If you check your heart rate regularly, its rate of change should give you an idea of how long your powers could keep you going. My running theory is that Soren's heart rate will likely diminish according to how strong the remaining radiation is."

"Well, that theory is still more than I had when I

came in," Soren responded.

"Honestly, if that guess is even within a hundred years, I'd be surprised," Orson said. "But I'll be long gone by the time you find out, I suppose."

"So Soren," Bea said. "I saw on the news they were talking about some glowing, flying person. Was that all you?"

Orson dismissed himself before Soren replied. "I haven't seen the stories, but it sounds about right," he answered, flashing a smile. "Were they talking about Milwaukee?"

"That was at first, then there were some stories that started surfacing from Nevada and from Missouri. They talk about you like you could be some kind of superhero."

"That, I've heard. What do you think?"

"I think that'd be crazy, but in a good way."

"That seems to be the consensus," he laughed. "I guess I should be getting on my way."

"Wait, where are you going?" Bea asked, concern in her voice.

"I've got to be back in Chicago by tonight. I'll probably be hanging around there for a bit."

"Will you be coming back?"

"Maybe sometime. I've got some things to take care of first."

"Well, if you do any more hero stuff, be careful. We already thought we lost you once," she said.

"I'll do my best," Soren reassured her, then he made his way back outside. At the end of the lane, he took one look back at the building as if trying to hold onto something nostalgic. But he forced himself to turn and rocket away, Chicago his next destination.

CHAPTER 07
MAKING A HERO

Chicago, Illinois
Saturday, August 21, 2027

Doctor Holst arrived in Chicago Saturday morning. Together, he and Soren found an apartment in which to stay for their duration in the city. Once they were settled in, Soren informed Holst about the additional tests he had had done. "Doctor Orson believes I could live almost as long as the half-life's duration. Maybe longer," he said as he concluded the story. "Personally, I don't know whether to wish for him to be right or wrong."

"That is an awfully long life to live," Holst agreed. "I have news as well. On my way here, I heard about a gang of sorts that has recently gone public. Reportedly, they call themselves 'Absolution'. They're a large group, but it's believed they don't spread beyond Chicago. Apparently, Chicago PD has had a lot of difficulty with them as of late."

"I take it you think I should start here by trying to take down some of these… gangsters?"

"I don't see why not."

"I mean, one thing that'd be helpful is knowing how to find them if we really are going to do this."

"That may be a little more difficult," Holst explained. "They're rather quiet with the exact nature of their actions. They leave just enough evidence to have a signature on their crimes. Beyond that, no one seems to know when or where they'll crop up, or who might be involved."

Soren sat in thought for a moment. "If no one else has been able to predict their movements, I doubt we could. But I suppose we can give it a try anyway. I need you to pull up records on all their actions since their first appearance. And get a read on the police radios in the area. If anything big happens, I want to know right away."

Holst beamed. "I'll have it ready in a minute."

And as promised, it was only sixty seconds before Holst had managed to obtain the radio signal and the necessary data. At present, radio chatter was silent. But the data on the gang was seemingly random. Mostly, its activities consisted of kidnappings, though occasionally they seemed to perform other crimes.

Missing people attributed to Absolution's actions seemed to be from all walks of life: a politician, a local zookeeper, a pharmacist, a university biology student, and a bank teller were among the known disappearances. As for other activities: two different store supply trucks had been hijacked, a family with a great amount of accumulated debt had turned up dead, and they had robbed one bank.

Connecting the various activities seemed impossible at first glance. Judging solely by the robberies they committed may have been just for supplies. The kidnapping victims were from such diverse backgrounds that nothing seemed to make sense. None of them had any known enemies or any major debts that they could have been searched for, nor did they have any religious, ethnic, genetic, or social connections in common.

It was in looking at the cargo of the trucks that had been hijacked that Soren found something odd. "One was carrying household chemicals, the other had prescription medicines," he pointed out. "If they were aiming for supplies, wouldn't they have gone for food at some point? But there's nothing about food."

"Good eye," Holst praised. "Do you think they're mass producing drugs?"

"It's possible, but look at who they've abducted. If they were choosing targets at random, they'd probably just be killing them. But these are kidnappings. And there's a pharmacist and a biology major among them. These are deliberately targeted individuals."

"So whatever they're making, they need the extra expertise. What about the zookeeper?"

"I'd say animal testing, but I somehow doubt they're that humane," Soren replied, deep in thought. "Even so—"

But he was cut off as a radio signal crackled in. At the same time, a siren sounded outside. "—in pursuit. Suspect heading south on North Broadway from International Bank. Requesting backup. Suspect armed and dangerous."

"I suppose that's my cue," Soren said, opening a window and rocketing through it. In seconds he had caught up to the chase, which already had three police cars in tow.

Soren flew down beside the car in question and was almost immediately greeted by a barrage of gunfire. He barrel rolled out of the way just in time, and the assault struck the brick wall of a building across the street instead. Realizing a direct assault on the gunman would be difficult in his current situation, Soren fell back slightly and directed a flare at the car's passenger rear tire.

The rubber melted and the hubcap glowed with heat just before the tire burst. The car began to skid, but its momentum was still quite great. Soren launched himself toward the intersection where an elderly woman was crossing right in the car's path. He swooped in and grabbed her just before the car passed the place she had been standing.

The vehicle spun to a halt in the middle of the intersection as police cars raced in to barricade all possible escapes. Policemen took up defensive positions as the gunman stumbled out the vehicle and began to open fire on them. Soren dropped in just as the gunfire began, and he projected a powerful electromagnetic field around the suspect.

The bullets became like a halo around the criminal before he realized what was happening and stopped firing. Soren released the field and the projectiles dropped harmlessly to the ground. He rushed at the now stupefied gunman and the two grappled over the firearm for a moment as Soren projected heat through its metal barrel. With a yelp of pain, the gunman released his grip and the weapon was in Soren's possession. Warily, the police began to make their way toward the two combatants.

Soren set the gun on the ground away from its owner as the perpetrator was apprehended. "He's all yours, officers. Oh, and be careful with that; it's hot," he said, gesturing toward the smoking firearm. Soren turned and launched away as spectators stared in awe. The confrontation had only lasted about a minute.

Soren further assisted the police in apprehending two additional criminals before the day was done. After the last, he soared to the top of a skyscraper and looked out over the sunset. If he continued to perform like he had today, it wouldn't be long before Bolton took notice of his actions.

Satisfied with the day's work, he returned to his and Holst's apartment. "The radio's been full of chatter about what you've done today. They, like the people in Milwaukee, are starting to call you a hero."

"I'm not doing it to be a hero, Doctor," Soren said. "I'm doing this to settle a score."

"Yes, well, I'd think he should reconsider trying to take down someone who has become an icon to so many people so quickly."

Soren grunted in response. He wasn't keen on the idea of being an icon in the way Holst seemed to think. "Any luck on figuring out the actions of that group, 'Absolution'?"

"Not yet. I've been trying to follow every lead and tip related to them, but so far, everything is coming up dead ends. They seem to be deliberate in covering up their tracks. I wonder if they're not just some lowly gang, but maybe something… more."

"Let me know if you do unearth anything,"

Soren requested. "I'm going to change, then it's bed for me."

The next two days had passed much as their first in Chicago had gone. Holst was stuck at a complete standstill in trying to discover anything about Absolution while Soren assisted the police where he could in taking down various criminals and rescuing those in danger, even helping a family escape a house fire on one occasion.

But at the end of his third day in the city, when Soren returned to the apartment, he found it ransacked. There had clearly been a struggle, and Doctor Holst was nowhere to be found. Soren looked over much of the doctor's equipment, and as far as he could tell, everything was still there, but he found the doctor's computer still on.

Soren shook the mouse to wake the computer from Sleep Mode. A paused video was pulled up on the screen, and when Soren clicked "play" he immediately saw the unfamiliar face of a man with fair skin and a black beard. When the face spoke, a Russian accent was thick in his deep voice.

"Doctor Grant," he began. "You and your friend have spent far too much time investigating the Absolution. Your friend, Doctor Holst, has proceeded much too far in his research, so ve have deleted all he has found that is vithin his machines. In tventy-four hours time, ve also plan to delete everything inside his brain.

"If you vish to prevent this, then ve offer a bargain: your life for his. Six o'clock, Tuesday evening. You vill find us in a varehouse on Vest Magnolia Avenue. If you present yourself, ve shall spare his life. If you do not, his life is forfeit.

"Oh, and Doctor. Do be sure to come alone, vill you? And of course, tell novun of this recording. If you do, vell, ve vouldn't vant things getting any… messier."

CHAPTER 08
UPGRADE

Washington, DC
Tuesday, August 24, 2027

Chrome gleamed in the dim lighting within the bunker nestled under the U.S. capitol. The machine to which it belonged stood over eight feet tall, and was roughly humanoid in shape. Its bulk comprised of various high-power weapons: a rocket attachment could be seen projected from its wrist, and two large plasma cannons sprouted from its shoulders. The hands could double as something akin to a fully-automatic rifle. Red and blue accents detailed the chrome surface, and stars adorned its chest.

As workers scurried around the mech, two figures stood atop a stretch of steel scaffolding overlooking the labor some distance back. One of the figures was a chiseled man wearing dress blues (which were tighter fitting and much more uncomfortable looking than the fatigues he usually donned), a glimmering badge upon his chest declaring his rank. His blonde hair was buzzed into a flat-top, his eyes sunken and his brows a formidable ridge. His jaw muscles were so taut one might wonder whether he could open his mouth at all.

His companion was a tall, poised woman with a commanding presence. Her eyes and hair were both dark in color, the latter drawn back into a tight bun. Her suit was adorned with a brooch that carried the U.S. Presidential Seal. She focused with pursed lips on the ongoing construction of the oversized robot before them.

As they watched, a scientist approached them, his scrawny knees barely seeming able to hold his own weight. He spoke with a squeaky voice as he addressed them, "Madam President. General Bolton," he said. "I bring a report."

"Proceed, Doctor," the woman permitted.

"Our team of scientists and engineers has worked tirelessly since the Star Buster has been returned to us. You will find that shield and armor efficiency are each up two hundred percent from its last use. Efficiency of movement is also up nearly three hundred percent, and power usage and efficiency have also been significantly improved. Lastly, you should find the controls to be more responsive.

"I believe," the squeaky-voiced scientist continued, "you will be pleased to know that we have met and exceeded project goals within the allotted time. Our men are putting the finishing touches on today, and it will be fully operational by tomorrow morning."

"Thank you, Doctor," the president said. "Dismissed."

The large man waited for the wiry-legged doctor to hurry away. "Madam President, if the report is to be believed, I have every confidence that the Star Buster is now capable of handling the mission it is required for."

President Isolde Sharpe remained silent in consideration for a moment before answering. She seemed much more cautious in her choice of words than her more rash associate. "You underestimate the mission, I believe, General Bolton. I did not promote you for you to underestimate your quarry."

She continued, "On the subject of quarries, we are running out of time. You must take care of Doctor Grant in less than a week, and given the information we now have, it would be immensely beneficial if you could get him here *alive*."

"I doubt he will respond well to my invitation given our history," Harold Bolton replied. "He doesn't seem fond of the military. A sin toward his own country."

"On the contrary, you may have been too forceful early on. But if I did not think you up for the job, I would not have promoted you. Please don't prove me wrong."

"Yes, Madam President," Bolton said. "Do we have any knowledge of his whereabouts?"

"Chicago, Illinois. It seems 'Quasar' has been trying his hand at some hero business there."

"Hero business, ma'am?"

"He is helping the local police fight crime as a sort of vigilante. The citizens sing his praises left and right as if he was their greatest wish come true. But, if he truly is a hero, he will be necessary in our mission. I should have begun looking for members for the Lodestar Project long ago. I only hope two will be enough.

"Bolton," she said, her formality melting into friendship, "we cannot risk you doing this mission alone. The Star Buster was designed primarily to handle nuclear weapons, but you are as aware as I am that what we are about to face has the potential to destroy the entire planet."

"Do you truly think Doctor Grant can make such a large difference?"

"It's not a matter of what I believe, General. It's a matter of what we have to do just for a chance of survival."

There was a moment of pause. "As you know," Bolton resumed, "I no longer have a family to protect, but I do have a country. The way I see it, that's just as important."

President Sharpe did not respond, but continued to stare straight ahead. Bolton continued, "I'll bring Doctor Grant back here, if you truly believe it improves our chances."

"I do."

"Then it will be done."

CHAPTER 09
ABSOLUTION

Chicago, Illinois
Tuesday, August 24, 2027

Sunset was drawing near as Soren sat perched atop a Comcast store on a corner opposite the designated warehouse that Absolution was using as a meeting point. From what he could see of the inside, the warehouse itself looked busy, as if many people were preparing to move out at any moment.

From his current position, he couldn't see if Doctor Holst was in the building or not. Regardless, he had to take his chance. It was time to barter for the life of his friend.

Soren flew across and hovered just below one of the high windows he had been watching through moments ago. He peered inside, and at last spotted Doctor Holst bound to a chair near the center of the nearly empty warehouse, his head low and what appeared to be a gag in his mouth.

He waited only a moment longer, and, while there seemed to be no one watching his position, he soared through the open window and landed a few yards from the captive Holst.

"Doctor Grant," a familiar Russian voice rang out. The man from the video skulked out of the shadows; he had been hiding in one of Soren's blind spots. "I knew you vould show up." He clicked his fingers at one of the men who had been moving supplies. "Bring us some vine, vould you? Ve must have drinks vhile ve... negotiate."

"There's nothing to negotiate, is there?" Soren asked as the underling disappeared. "I showed up, just as you asked. Now your end of the bargain is to release Doctor Holst."

The man clucked four times. "I am seeing you do not undorstand the intricacies of this business, Doctor Grant. Especially vhen ve must deal vith somevun of *your* caliber.

"See, you are a very powerful individual, Doctor. Ve must deal vith you carefully so that ve do not find ourselves being double-crossed."

The man returned with two full glasses of wine and handed one each to Soren and the man who seemed to be in charge. Then two others produced folding metal chairs for them to each sit in. As the black-bearded man sat, he addressed Soren. "Sit, Doctor. Make yourself comfortable."

Soren warily looked around the room before he sat. He didn't like the idea of lowering his guard in a dangerous situation like this. The man in front of him drank deeply. When he realized Soren had not taken so much as a sip, he spoke again. "Drink. Ve vould not poison you. I have my doubts for it vurking on an enhanced porson like you anyvay." He took another sip, then added, "Besides, it vould be less fun than vot I have planned."

"I'm fine, thanks," Soren replied, though he was tempted. His throat and mouth were parched—his nerves were getting to him.

"You decline our hospitality. Not a vise decision, Doctor," he said, taking another swig from his glass and smacking his lips. "I am realizing I have not introduced myself. Forgive my rudeness. I am called Victor. I am understanding that for your people that is vot you call somevun who vins. Fitting, as I intend to come out on top here today." He chuckled, but Soren remained silent.

"The quiet type, eh?" Victor prodded. "That must change soon. Vot insurance do ve have that you vill not manage to escape us?"

"I showed up, and despite my instincts, I didn't incinerate you on sight."

Victor began guffawing so loudly Soren thought the glass in the Russian's hand must be near shattering from the sound waves. "Ve have you outnumbered, Doctor. Brute force vould not have vorked. And yes, ve are avare that simple gunfire von't vork on you either. You seem to magnetize modern bullets. But ve have other weapons at our disposal."

"So why the delay? If you are capable of what you say, then certainly you don't need to wait."

"Ve have been considering this, but vhile ve desire your demise, ve also do not vont things getting messy. Nor do ve vish for a spectacle, Doctor. Ve have decided that the best way to do avay vith you is through the use of non-magnetic tools. Have you ever heard of the legends of vampires?"

Soren nodded slowly, a look of skepticism upon his face.

"Ve have decided to dispose of you much like the legendary vampire. A vooden stake you cannot repel vill be driven through your heart. You vill be positioned such that all blood vill be drained from your body vithout so much mess to clean lator."

Soren hadn't planned out any possible escapes prior to his arrival, mostly due to not knowing what might lie in store for him when he got here. But here his captor was, explaining each detail, and gears were turning in Soren's head, formulating his escape. At the description of Soren's planned demise, however, Holst finally began fighting at his bonds and shouting against the gag fixed into his mouth.

"Oh, Doctor Holst, I almost forgot you vere here," Victor said. "Vell, as that seems to have found favor vith the old man, ve may as vell proceed vith the plan. Bind him," Victor commanded, gesturing at Soren.

Two men approached and bound his hands in what at first seemed to be normal cloth. He would have fought back, if not for Holst being in such close proximity. He couldn't risk hurting his friend. "Flame-retardant fabric," Victor specified, describing the unusual shackles that bound Soren. "Von't make it easy for you to escape." Two others carried a table—a hole had been cut in it to let Soren's blood through—to a spot only a short distance to Doctor Holst's right. As they did, the men who had bound Soren's wrists were now fitting a gag to him. Yet another man brought a bucket and placed it under the hole in the table.

Soren was pushed and shoved to the table and laid with his head up. He looked over at Doctor Holst, a look of horror in the old man's eyes. Soren's arms and legs were each bound to a leg of the table, and when they had finished, Victor approached, a wooden stake in his hand.

"Oh, I forgot vun last thing, Doctors. Ve can't have vitnesses to our activities," he said, snatching the bucket from underneath Soren and moving it to directly in front of Doctor Holst's seat. Soren at last began to struggle as he realized what was coming and focused energy toward his extreme joints. Flame-retardant didn't mean completely fire-proof. He just had to get past that burning point. No need to worry yet. "I vill have to take back my vord about exchanging lives. Many apologies, Doctor Grant."

The next moment passed in slow motion for Soren. Victor grabbed the back of Holst's head and positioned the stake directly over the bucket, its point upright. Try as he might, he couldn't quite seem to reach the burning point for the material that kept his hands and feet stretched out at his sides. Panic finally began to set in. He wasn't heating up fast enough to break free. His bonds began to smoke, but would not catch flame. Soren screamed, "NO!" but against his gag, his voice was unintelligible. Then in one move, Holst was forced forward and Soren closed his eyes, hearing the stake meet the soft flesh of Holst's neck.

Soren began to shake from anger and sorrow— anger not just at Victor for his lies, but at himself for believing it, and for failing to do the one thing that he had managed with such ease in recent days. He had lost his long-standing friend and mentor. At this moment, his concern was not for his own life. He only desired to make these thugs feel some amount of the pain he felt in this moment.

"Towel, please," Victor asked one of his men,

and moments later, he heard the Russian's footsteps growing closer. Soren felt his emotions reaching a boiling point. But then he felt it. He realized his anger had built up a large amount of heat and energy inside him. Even to him, holding it much longer might be dangerous, but still he held it. He had one chance. His breathing slowed. Victor's footsteps grew closer. He heard the bucket clink on the ground. He could feel Victor's alcohol-tinged breath on him. "Good-bye, Doctor Grant," he said.

Soren's eyes at last snapped open, and a burst of heat unlike any he had ever before created exploded from his very being. The cloth binding him burst into flame and was consumed instantly. He heard people and objects smash against walls and against the few crates still left sitting there. A couple of people screamed.

Some of the bodies that had been launched from his vicinity had caught fire. Most of them lay motionless, and Soren could only assume they were dead. Victor's body in particular was twisted at odd angles, lying face-down on the concrete floor. Someone lunged at Soren, but he raised his hand and another blast emanated from his palm. His assailant was launched forcefully backward, and when he came to a halt, he lay still.

Another thug was getting desperate and had grabbed a belt of grenades from a broken crate and was pulling a pin from one as Soren threw a fireball that caused the entire belt to erupt. One after another, Soren launched fireballs at the various survivors of Absolution. Some missed and struck crates or the walls of the massive building, causing more flames to spring to life in their wake.

In only a minute's time, the entire building was engulfed in flames. Soren heard sirens approaching, and with the roar of fire echoing around him, there was no certainty just how far away they were. Without looking back, Soren flew from the scene heading out over the Chicago River and into the sky. Holst was gone, and there was no bringing him back.

He flew out and away from Chicago, where to, he didn't care. The sun had nearly set by the time he had left the scene. Below, street lights began to flicker on, cars had lit their headlamps, and no one was the wiser that a great scientist had just perished, or that a dangerous gang had been snuffed out.

Soren rocketed over Lake Michigan, his insides still twisting, his mind still numb. His rage had left him; Victor, with whom he had been furious at, no longer lived to direct any anger at. Instead, he was nearly drowned by the weight of his own grief. Fitting, he thought, as he hovered over the Great Lake.

He allowed himself to drop slowly in altitude until he was just inches from the water. He considered letting himself drop in as he watched the last sliver of the sun disappear over the horizon. He would be snuffed out, just like that sunlight. He'd never have to feel this pain again. He shouldn't even be alive right now to think these thoughts, so why was he hesitating?

At that moment, his mind wandered to the old lady he had saved his first night in Chicago, the look of gratitude on her face. Then to the young boy he had saved from falling off a bridge after losing control of his bike. Then to the store owner he had brought stolen groceries back to after apprehending the criminal. Even more faces flashed through his mind as a tear escaped him, only to evaporate while still fresh on his cheek.

There were still those who looked up to him. They thought he was a hero. But would they still think the same of him after he had gone into a blind rage and killed dozens of people, even if those people were dangerous criminals?

Soren turned and looked at the lights of the city, smoke still rising from the warehouse that had now been burned to the ground. Surely the city would get on without him, right? Or the world for that matter. People didn't need superheroes. They survived when those heroes were only myths, so what would change now?

A small boat passed by, but he tried to pay it no mind. He continued staring down at the water of the lake, stars and city lights reflected in its glassy surface. The only disturbance to the mirror-like image was occasional bobbing or rippling.

Then Soren realized the boat had stopped, and two people were standing near the edge of the deck, waving to him. He floated closer, and he heard the much shorter figure saying in an excited voice, "That's him! That's the man who saved me on the bridge, daddy!"

Meanwhile, the taller man beckoned for Soren to come closer. Soren wasn't sure why, but he did what he was asked in that moment. "Hey, so you're the one the news has been calling 'Quasar', right?" the dad asked as Soren drew near. Soren simply nodded in response. It seemed a strange question to ask.

The dad continued. "I never got to thank you for saving my son the other day. Had you not been in the neighborhood while he was out riding with his friends, he—he might not have, you know, made it." He seemed to be choking back tears of his own.

"I just wanted to say, I know you're a—a superhero and all, but if there's anything you might need—"

The son interrupted, "Daddy, super guy looks sad. Why does super guy look sad?"

Soren felt water evaporating from his eyes. "I—I lost a friend of mine today," he choked. "I couldn't save him." Soren again felt compelled to be honest despite himself.

"But you're super guy!" the boy cheered. "If you couldn't do it, there musta been a really bad guy that done it." The dad looked stunned, but neither he nor Soren made to discourage the child.

"There was," Soren said, sitting on the edge of the boat's deck.

"But you got the bad guy, right? You beat him up?"

Soren's voice caught. "I—yeah, I—I beat him."

"Then that's a good thing ain't it? Right, daddy? 'Cause that means he can't hurt anyone else, right?"

Of all the things in the world, Soren hadn't counted on the innocence of a young child to help him see the light in his loss.

"Sometimes," Soren croaked, "even when the good guys win, it still feels like a loss."

"That just means you gotta win even better next time, right?" the boy chimed. "And I know you can do it, 'cause you're super guy. You can't lose. You're gonna save a lot more people. I know you are."

Maybe Soren had been wrong, or maybe the kid was wrong, but Soren decided to take a chance on the optimism of that young boy. He wouldn't give up today. In that moment, that child had become his hero.

CHAPTER 10
STAR VS MACHINE

Chicago, Illinois
Wednesday, August 25, 2027

Soren was out of the apartment early the next morning. The previous day's events still weighed on his mind, but he had made his decision with the help of that boy. He would continue to be a hero to those in need.

Or at least he would if anyone actually needed saving. But so far, nothing seemed to be happening. No sirens sounded, no loud shouting echoed from the streets below. Everything actually seemed peaceful. Thus, he decided to drop to ground level and perhaps, despite the knot still in his stomach, he would attempt a breakfast.

He stopped in a local bakery and thought of ordering a chocolate donut in hopes that the natural stimulants in the chocolate might help boost his mood. When he reached the counter, the cashier seemed giddy. "Hey, it's Quasar! Don't worry, your order's on the house today."

Soren was taken aback. "What? No, I can pay, it's perfectly fine."

"Nonononono," the cashier said quickly. "I heard the news. Everyone's heard the news. That awful gang, Absolution, was taken down last night. Word on the street says you're the one that did it. I owed money to one of their guys, and they were threatening to take my family away. My family is still alive because of you. So yes, your order's on the house. Today, and everyday if you want."

Soren didn't bother arguing after that. It seemed that everywhere he went that morning, everyone began whispering excitedly about him. A couple of people even asked for pictures. He hardly felt like the actions from the previous day should earn him celebrity status. If anything, he thought people would be afraid of him if they associated him with the burning of that warehouse.

Instead, more people than usual seemed to be vying for attention, and he had never wanted the spotlight less. Eventually, he elected to fly to the top of the Willis Tower to overlook the city. Planes passed overhead as the sun rose higher into the sky. Traffic passed below in better order than normal, and still, it seemed to be an oddly peaceful day.

One airplane caught his eye. Even distant and on the eastern horizon, it appeared to be a rather odd shape. Maybe it was just a trick of the light. Then Soren realized it was actually heading straight toward Chicago, and decided it must simply be the angle he was looking from. Somehow his perspective distorted the view.

But closer and closer it drew, and Soren still thought it looked awfully odd. Then it dawned on him that it was flying quite low, and that brought about the realization that plane or not, something was wrong, so he rocketed out intending to meet it.

He finally came to the conclusion that this flying object was not a plane, but it also wasn't some rocket that had been launched at Chicago, either. It was too misshapen for that. Yet somehow it felt familiar. Regardless, if it meant ill, Soren would do everything in his power to stop it.

Soon it became evident that the familiar feeling

was not without cause. Soren had indeed seen this object before. However, it had also undergone some small changes. But it wasn't a plane; it wasn't a rocket; it wasn't an alien spacecraft, either. It was a burly machine, eight-and-a-half feet tall, kitted with weapons of all different types.

It was the Star Buster flying toward him, its fresh coat of paint gleaming in the midday sun.

Soren had at one point been intending to lure it and its pilot back to fight, but this felt like the most inopportune time for it to reappear. Even so, he didn't intend to lose this time, regardless of recent events. If anything, he intended to let the remainder of his emotions fly during the impending combat. Bolton would for once come in handy, even if it was as a punching bag.

"Caught back up to me, have you?" Soren said, a bit of anger rising in his voice as he drew level with the machine.

"Doctor Grant, I am on a time sensitive mission to bring you back to the capitol," Bolton's voice echoed over the lake hundreds of feet below them.

"Why's that, so you can experiment on me again? I've already found out everything I need to about my condition," he said. "No thanks to having to watch over my shoulder for your ugly mug."

"You misunderstand, Doctor Grant."

"Do I?" Soren snapped. "Anytime you've shown up your goal has been to either capture or kill! I'm not some science experiment or pet for you to keep in a cage!"

"Doctor, that is not the goal this time."

"This time? So you admit to it! Sorry if I've been tricked one too many times lately, but I'm not about to buy into it."

"I should warn you before you go any further," Bolton explained, "that this suit has been upgraded substantially since we last met, and I do not wish to have to use it on you."

"Why'd you bring it then? If you're really trying to avoid a confrontation, why would you bring the biggest gun you've got? I don't care how many upgrades you've given that thing, I'm taking it down this time."

"Doctor—" Bolton started, but Soren had already launched toward the suit, putting out the strongest magnetic field he could muster. The engines keeping the Star Buster aloft began to sputter as Soren barraged the armor with blasts of heat, the shields having been quickly disabled by the near equivalent of an electromagnetic pulse detonation that Soren had created.

The duo plummeted toward Lake Michigan, and Soren could hear Bolton frantically trying to get the Star Buster to properly respond again. At last, he got an arm to work and it swatted Soren away almost like a fly. The Star Buster became operational again only just before hitting the water. The tips of its overlarge feet splashed against the lake before the machine properly stabilized. Soren also regained his balance just as the Star Buster began rising into the air once more.

Soren launched himself again toward the machine, his fury boiling his insides, but he was too late to regain the upper hand. The Star Buster's hands raised in front of it, and a fusillade of bullets rained from its fingertips. Soren dodged to his right just as he realized what was coming his way; he then spiraled around the Star Buster, slowly getting nearer as he took advantage of the greater speed he had over the machine.

Bolton seemed to have realized this, however, as one of the Star Buster's shoulder-mounted cannons pivoted in Soren's direction and launched a blast of plasma directly in his path. Narrowly, Soren avoided the blast by diving beneath it. He used this as his line of attack and continued under its feet as Bolton fumbled to find a means of catching his nimble opponent. As he passed beneath, orbs of green flame flashed from Soren's hands and collided with the legs of the Star Buster. To his relief, the shields still appeared to be down when the flames found their mark and glowed white-hot.

Bolton cursed loudly and the Star Buster wheeled around and a large hand again swung at Soren, but he again managed to evade by a hair's breadth, swerving up and away from the massive appendage. Unfortunately, this had once more created distance between him and his quarry. Two more plasma discharges missed due to Soren's superior maneuverability, and the distance between them extended even further.

Bolton took his chance and released a batch of small rockets from the mech's wrist. Again, Soren barrel rolled out of harm's way, but realized as the projectiles soared past him that they must be heat-seeking missiles in some form, because they turned around and came after him again.

Soren rocketed off, leading them on a chase, but knowing that he was invariably the largest heat signature in the area, they would hound him endlessly if he didn't find something to do with them. Then, to make matters worse, Bolton began taking full advantage of the situation by unleashing another barrage of gunfire from the Star Buster's fingertips.

Without being able to slow down, Soren couldn't logically use his own projectiles to stop the missiles. Yet if he didn't find a way to lose them, he'd end up a crispy treat for the fish in the lake. He did the only thing he knew to do: he sped up. While he did so, he generated a magnetic field around himself that he hoped would be enough to dispel Bolton's bullets.

He weaved and rolled through the sky, trying to find a proper chance to get in closer to the Star Buster. At last he led the missiles directly away from Bolton, who had to cease firing to avoid accidentally prematurely detonating the missiles. Then, in the most difficult airborne trick he had performed to date, Soren doubled back in an extremely tight u-turn that the missiles couldn't perfectly follow.

As Soren flew straight for the Star Buster—the missiles lagging more behind than ever—Bolton began to fire at him once more. Soren dodged narrowly under the arm of the machine, realizing as he passed that Bolton had managed to bring the Star Buster's shields back online.

Even with that drawback, the stunt brought about the desired result. The heat-seeking missiles collided with the Star Buster, unable to maneuver as well as Soren had. Almost instantly, the explosions depleted the entirety of Bolton's recently-restored shields. Soren took his own chance at this moment and bombarded the back of the giant machine with jets of bright flame.

The armor glowed as the viridian fire roared and lapped against it. Bolton yelled in pain from within. Soren's goal was not to kill his foe, but if he created some extra scarring, he wasn't going to feel guilty. Soren became so focused on his assault that he didn't notice the two shoulder cannons pivoting around to face him until too late.

Two great plasma bolts greeted Soren as he attempted to create a shield of heat and magnetism to stop them, but this time, he was too slow and his attempted defense too feeble. The assault met its mark and Soren was sent tumbling through the air. Pain seared in his chest and across his right side as he attempted to find his balance again, but it was a massive effort just to maintain consciousness.

Soren splashed into the lake and felt bubbles rise around him as the energy he was still putting out boiled the water in contact with his skin. He squinted upward, seeing the sun refracted through the lake. Despite his effort, he couldn't right himself to escape from what was sure to be his watery grave.

Then, to confirm his fears, a shadow obscured the last of the sun's rays that he was sure to see. The shadow drew nearer. Bolton was coming to deliver the final blow. He surely wouldn't allow Soren to get off as easily as drowning in his final moments. He saw one of the great hands of the

Star Buster break through the water, reaching toward him.

And Soren was sputtering, breathing the cold Lake Michigan air again. He had been lifted out of the water and was being carried in the arms of the Star Buster. He felt humiliated; his enemy was now his rescuer. Except there was no way he was being taken anywhere other than a lab or a prison cell. Either way, as his consciousness faded, he was sure he would spend the rest of his days locked up, never to see daylight again.

Soren was flying through the sky. A brilliant meteor of quasinium was falling toward earth, and he was there to witness it, right by its side. He seemed to talk to it, and oddly, it talked back. It had no face or mouth to speak through, yet its answers seemed to be coming through Soren's mind. The conversation seemed empty, consisting only of unintelligible syllables, but eventually something seemed to come into focus.

The meteor's voice was telling him that his

powers had been a mistake. He was an accident, nothing more. Then Soren realized that the meteor's voice was actually Holst's voice, telling Soren how he had failed. He said that Quasar could never be a hero to the world. He had failed to defeat Bolton, and had failed to save Holst's life.

The Holst-meteor crashed into the ground, and suddenly Soren was back in the burning warehouse, the bodies of the Absolution's thugs in disfigured piles around him, but one figure stood out most of all: the charred and limp body of Hardwin Holst.

Soren let out a cry, and he was suddenly bombarded with the voices of so many people taunting him, as the corpses of people he knew rose from the flames around him. Victor, Bolton, Orson, Bea, Holst, the boy from the boat, and so many others. He was being shaken by an endless sea of people who he had harmed, and endless more who would likely one day join them.

"Soren, Soren, Soren," the voices echoed. Then he awoke.

Soren awoke with a start. Indeed, someone had been saying his name and shaking him, though much more gently than he had felt in the nightmare. His nurse looked at him with fear in her eyes. "You were yelling in your sleep, and trembling horribly," she said. "Must have been some nightmare."

A new wave of embarrassment washed over him. To have been discovered in the midst of such a childish nightmare by a complete stranger, nurse or no, felt like the epitome of humiliation. Soren looked around. He seemed to be in a normal hospital, despite his prior expectations. A clock on the wall read 6:47 P.M.

"How long was I out," Soren asked groggily.

"About 30 hours," she told him.

"Where am I?"

"BridgePoint Hospital. North side of Capitol Hill."

"Capitol Hill? You mean like next to the White House?" Soren asked, not sure he had heard the nurse properly.

"The one and the same. You have some friends in high places."

"I do? That's news to me," Soren said.

"Mhm. I was ordered to let them know as soon as you were ready to talk."

"Ordered? Who would order you to let me talk to them."

"The President," she said with a giggle. "I knew you had gained some admirers with your work in Chicago, but I didn't expect it to have gone quite so high."

"Wait, you mean Isolde Sharpe is *here?*"

"Yep! So should I send her in?"

Soren's mouth went painfully dry almost immediately. What was he in for? He had assaulted a military officer. Would the President be seeking to determine his punishment directly? Would he get a trial? He had no idea what was coming if the President wanted to see him, but he dared not keep the President waiting.

"Sure," he said hesitantly, and the nurse turned

and left the room.

CHAPTER 11
MISSION BRIEFING

Washington, DC
Friday, August 27, 2027

President Sharpe's presence was just as impressive in person as it was on television, if not more. She entered Soren's room with purpose in her every step. "Doctor Grant," she addressed him with a curt nod. "Or should I call you Quasar? I hear that is the name the people call you now, all spawned from a person named Jim you met in Nevada, if I'm not mistaken?"

Soren swallowed hard, but he gulped only air. He did his best to not look intimidated. "M-Madam President, an—an honor to meet you in person," he said nervously. He wasn't sure if the question as to what she should call him was rhetorical or not, but when she took a moment to continue speaking, he realized it may not have been. Even so, her stern gaze never once faltered or broke.

"As I understand it, you are the cause for much

of the damage our Star Buster has sustained, are you not?" she asked.

This was it, Soren thought as he met her cold eyes. "I was," he said, trying to sound braver than he sounded in the face of such authority.

For a moment before President Sharpe turned from him, he thought he saw a smile crack her otherwise impregnable poker face. "I'm sure you know, it would take an individual of astounding abilities to damage such a piece of equipment. The Star Buster, though much of the public remains unaware of its existence, is designed to combat nuclear weapons. Its armor and shielding are enough to withstand the blast of a nuclear explosion.

"However," she continued, turning back toward him, the smile he imagined now gone, "As you may have discovered for yourself, it is also capable of being an effective anti-infantry or anti-aircraft weapon as well."

Soren nodded his understanding.

"Thankfully, even with the damage you caused it, our engineers have been able to restore it to its previous state with haste. Also thankfully, the doctors here have been congratulated on restoring both yourself and General Bolton to health."

Soren subdued his surprise. So Bolton had been promoted. Piloting the Star Buster must have had something to do with it. He sat up and asked, "Wait, you're thankful that *I'm* in good health? What importance can my well-being be to you?"

"A great deal of importance, Doctor Grant," she replied. "I regret heavily that you and General Bolton came to blows. I feel that he and you got off on the wrong foot, and I worry that I may be in part to blame for that, as the general was only ever acting on my orders, whether directly or otherwise. Though he seemed to take a more violent approach to his orders when it pertained to you after your escape. I believe he took that first encounter personally."

Soren looked down at his feet. "I may have been a little hotheaded myself," he admitted. He felt almost like a child being told by his parents that they were disappointed in something he had done.

"I won't contradict you," President Sharpe said, pulling a chair close to his bed and taking a seat. "However, there was fault on both sides, and I would be greatly appreciative if you would accept my apology, as there is another matter of paramount importance I need to discuss with you."

Soren looked up, "Of course, Madam President. And I'd be happy to help, if I can."

"Excellent. I'm afraid that the details of this matter are highly confidential, so I will need to have you transmitted to a more proper location for further briefing. Would you be willing to join me in the Oval Office along with General Bolton within the hour?"

Soren blinked twice quickly. He had just been invited inside the White House by the President. "Of course," he said, trying not to sound too shocked or excited.

"Good. I will arrange for your discharge and escort. Unless, of course," she shot him a grin, "you'd rather fly on your own terms?"

Soren considered her offer for a moment. Being escorted into the White House by security like some guest of honor would certainly be the opportunity of a lifetime, but then, a delegate from any nation could get treatment like that, right? How many people could actually fly straight to the White House like he would be able to do?

"I think I'll fly. Feels a bit more free that way," he replied, not entirely truthful about the things he was thinking.

"Then I will be certain your escort meets you in the front lawn when you arrive. Don't be late," she smiled, and made for the door. With her hand on the knob, she turned back to him. "Oh, I almost forgot. It is my understanding that you were the first to discover a unique metallic substance within these recent meteors. As such, the honor should truly go to you for the opportunity to name this substance. Have you, perchance, chosen a name for it?"

Soren felt sorrow strike at him again. "It's not exactly a name I came up with. Doctor Holst called it quasinium before he died. He named it after he heard what Bolton's team referred to me as while I was being held in the bunker."

"Oh, yes, I had heard of Doctor Holst's passing. I'm very sorry for your loss, Doctor Grant. But I thank you for this information."

After that, President Sharpe left the room. A minute later, the nurse had returned to tell Soren he was free to go. Soren climbed out of bed, vertigo a near instant companion, but after a moment, the dizziness cleared and, after changing into a set of normal clothing, he made his way from the hospital.

Soren took a deep breath of fresh air, not realizing until he was outside just how much he had been looking forward to it. Then, energy rippling from his hands and feet, he rocketed into the air and flew off toward the White House as he had been requested.

He landed in the front lawn of the White House to the sound of applause from various passersby. A trio of Secret Service members met him shortly after his arrival, and he was escorted into the capitol building. They brought him to the Oval Office, where he was ushered in and the door closed behind him.

Inside, he found Harold Bolton and Isolde Sharpe already present. "Nice entrance," Bolton said tersely. "Truce?" He extended a knotted hand.

"Truce," Soren responded and accepted the handshake. He had expected Bolton's grip to be firm, but something told him that the chiseled man was intentionally putting a fair bit more pressure into it than necessary, so Soren flashed a bit of heat from his palm in kind, but only enough that he knew it would give Bolton a slight stinging sensation.

As they released their near-standoff of a handshake and turned back to President Sharpe, she finally spoke. "Good. I'm about to need you two to work together, and it is of the utmost importance that you do. So, if you're ready for the details?"

Soren and Bolton both nodded and grunted affirmatives.

"Bolton already knows the basis, but Doctor Grant, for your benefit, I will begin from the top.

"The recent meteor showers that you were studying, Doctor, were but a precursor to something larger. These were apparently once fragments of a much more sizable body: an extinction-level meteor, much like the one hypothesized to have ended the dinosaurs.

"The mineral within this asteroid is, of course, the same quasinium that its predecessors contained. As you both already know from experience, quasinium contains radiation, and I can't pretend an impact coupled with radiation by a meteor this size would just give us all super powers like it seemed to have done for you, Doctor. And the fallout would easily spread for thousands of miles, not to mention it's plenty large enough to knock the planet off its axis.

"This meteor, if it continues on its same trajectory, would likely land somewhere in the upper parts of the northern hemisphere—possibly high enough that the heat it emits could melt the northern polar ice cap in minutes and cause torrential flooding worldwide. It'd be optimistic to assume human-kind could survive even one of the catastrophes this meteor threatens us with, but put them all together, and we stand no chance.

"It is for this reason that I must turn to individuals of extraordinary ability in order to stop this meteor from making landfall. As it turns out, the pilot of the Star Buster and the sole survivor of an explosive meteor impact are the only such people I have access to.

"I will not pretend that what I am asking of you will be a safe excursion. One or both of you could perish. But you are the only people who can destroy such a meteor. Using nuclear weapons would be too dangerous, putting nuclear radiation into the air, and if we do nothing, humanity as we know it will be wiped from the planet.

"So it is with great regret that I ask you both to lay down your lives not only for your neighbors or for your country, but for your entire planet. You are our only hope."

Silence fell between the three of them as President Sharpe's words sunk in. Bolton turned to Soren. "She already has my answer, but so you hear it as well: I've no family left. Never married, parents are gone, and I was an only child. I have no reason to refuse this mission. Live or die, I'll do it serving my country. I'm already in. The president doesn't think one person alone can do it."

"I'm *hoping* two of you can, but even then I have my concerns," President Sharpe added.

"Right," Bolton continued. "So it's up to you to decide the fate of this mission, Quasar."

It was Bolton's first time using the title without dissent. Soren was taken aback. Gathering his voice, he said, "I suppose if luck was against me, I should have died sometime in the last month. If this does kill me, I'll have gone full-circle. But, if I am going to die, I might as well make sure it's something worth dying for."

President Sharpe's stern countenance softened. She almost looked relieved. "Thank you, Quasar," she said. "And on that subject, you may be wondering why the suit you had worn before has not yet been returned to you. Our scientists have, forgive me, been working on upgrading it."

She paged someone, and one of the Secret Service men brought in a suitcase, set it before Soren, and exited again, closing the door and leaving them in privacy once more. When Soren hesitated, President Sharpe urged him, "Go on; open it."

Soren did as he was told, and he couldn't stifle the gasp that followed. Whether this new suit used elements from the one crafted by Doctor Holst or not, Soren could not tell by looking.

It was similar in ways to Holst's original design,

but without the armor. Midnight blue was the primary color across the majority of the suit. Chrome color lined the sleeves and legs, a gold-like trim creating a border between the chrome and dark blue. A diamond of chrome on the chest —similarly trimmed in gold—contained a familiar emblem: a gold galaxy-like spiral, slashed like a "Q".

"We realized your old suit was not as efficient as it could have been," President Sharpe explained. "I'm told this new model is layered in such a way as to make the armor obsolete. It should grant you further freedom of movement, while still improving your control over your powers just the same as the old version, if not even better. The mission I'm sending you on is certainly a superhero's mission. I'd be remiss if I didn't send you in as prepared as possible."

Soren stared at the new suit, dumbfounded. "Thank you," he managed to croak out. Slowly, he closed the suitcase back.

"One last detail. The meteoroid has an ETA of Sunday at midday. We set out for Nevada in the morning for you to prepare for the mission."

CHAPTER 12
SOARING TO HEAVEN

Secret Military Base, Nevada
Saturday, August 28, 2027

Soren joined General Bolton and President Sharpe on Air Force One the next morning. Together, the three were flown to Nevada, and Soren recognized the location as the same as the base he had once escaped from. He remembered that when he had escaped, there was no civilization for miles around.

As it turned out, the idea of "preparing for the mission" was testing Soren's ability to blast through various materials in various quantities. Boulders, blocks of solid steel, concrete walls (which went even better than his first-ever attempt on this site), and even small quantities of quasinium gathered from meteor impact sites.

None of the tests laid before him caused him any difficulty. Interestingly, when he attempted to flare energy toward quasinium, they found that the mineral exploded when exposed to high levels of similar radiation. Apparently, it could only hold a very specific amount of radiation and energy without volatile blasts resulting from within.

This discovery seemed to lighten the mood significantly. If the large meteor of quasinium responded just like the small ores, there would be a chance of it exploding easily when combated by Soren. For the first time since Soren had met her, President Sharpe actually seemed hopeful about the mission.

When it was at last decided that Soren had proven his abilities satisfactorily, he was allowed to rest for the evening. In the morning, he and Bolton were to be deployed to destroy the meteor.

Secret Military Base, Nevada
Sunday, August 29, 2027

Bolton—encased in the Star Buster armor—and Soren—wearing his new quasinium-amplifying suit—stood in the morning sun in the desert of

Nevada, awaiting the command to begin the mission. Bolton would be receiving directions on the Star Buster's heads-up display as to the quickest and most efficient way to strike the meteor.

The meteor's position was being tracked by all manner of tools, and the duo were to take flight well before it entered the atmosphere so that when it did enter, they would be there to stop it. The higher it was when they met it, the better chance they had of destroying it before it hit the ground.

Soren himself was wearing an earpiece so as to be able to better hear Bolton, as well as receive verbal commands from the command center. Apparently hundreds of scientists had been stationed all over the United States to track the meteor. They were even tracking Soren and Bolton to be sure of their position and actions, and to be able to provide direction if it was needed. Yet it would be President Sharpe issuing all commands during this mission; the command center would provide her with the necessary information, and she would filter the noise down to something the two could understand.

The command to fly came when the sun was still low on the horizon; barely an inch seemed to separate the two. President Sharpe's voice sounded over Soren's earpiece, "Ten seconds. Nine, eight, seven, six, five, four, three… Godspeed, gentlemen." Bolton rocketed into the air first, Soren following close behind. The two quickly reached mach speeds, their heading, northwest.

Never before had Soren flown so fast, nor had he needed to. He was partially aided by a slipstream created by following the bulk of the Star Buster, whose rocket systems were top-of-the-line. Once, Soren took a glimpse of the world below him. He had expected to see everything growing smaller as their altitude increased, but the change in size was made nearly indiscernible when compared to the blur of everything passing by.

Within a relatively short time, they had begun to pass over the Pacific Ocean, and it wasn't long after that before another mass of land that Soren was able to recognize as the southern part of Alaska was visible to them. Higher still they climbed, higher than Soren had gone before, and he suddenly wondered if he would be able to breathe in the upper atmosphere. After a moment, he realized that breathing at high speeds and high altitudes didn't seem to be a problem for him. Everything was the same as if he had been on the ground—another beneficial side effect of his powers, it seemed.

Then he saw it as they drew high enough in the sky for the atmosphere to begin losing its brilliant blues. The meteor was approaching, and while they had arrived ahead of time, the large rock was wasting no time in coming their way. It was easily the size of an Egyptian pyramid, if not larger. A metallic sheen glimmered off of various portions of its surface, broken by brown and gray expanses of rock.

Bolton was first to act, deploying from the Star Buster a number of machines that appeared similar to drones. The devices flew toward the meteor, their intent to slow it down to buy Soren and Bolton as much additional time as they could. Then, together, the two rained a fusillade of missiles, fireballs, and bursts of plasma into the rock.

Explosions littered the surface, but it showed no signs of breaking apart just yet. While the drones had succeeded in slowing it down in some capacity, it did not halt completely, and it picked up additional speed the closer it drew to Earth.

Soon, it met Soren and Bolton physically, the two pushing against it as it forced its way toward the surface. Never did the two falter in barraging the meteor with everything they could muster. The meteor trembled and cracks began to appear on its surface, yet it still did not break apart.

"It's... not... working!" Bolton yelled against the strain.

Soren simply focused on blasting the surface for a moment before it struck him. "Bolton!" he shouted. "Remember when we first met? Remember how I escaped the bunker?"

"How... is that... relevant?"

"I can drill to the center of this thing! Then you can use your missiles to destroy it from the inside!"

Bolton seemed to hesitate for a moment. "Alright! Do it!" he shouted at last, and Soren put everything he had into melting and blasting a hole to the center of the meteor. While the rock became liquid around his hands pressed to the already hot surface of the meteor, the metal exploded in their presence.

Soren was again reminded of his escape from the bunker with the explosions raining around him like fireworks as he bored his way deeper and deeper into the meteor. The hole that formed around him was much larger than himself due in part to the quasinium's own reactions. But Soren was also putting out a large amount of radiation from every part of his body.

Unlike the concrete of the bunker, however, Soren's progress was much faster this time. His powers had been honed a great deal since then. He no longer had to calculate his energy output like he had then. Instead, the action came almost as second nature. And before he knew it, he had forged a hole completely through the meteor.

"Bolton! It's clear!" Soren shouted flying behind the space rock now. Then he saw their relationship to the ground. Optimistically, they had seconds until impact.

Bolton flew to the center of the hole Soren created, and Soren protested. "I thought you were going to use the missiles!"

"Can't!" Bolton replied. "Out of ammo! I've got only one way to do this! Madam President, I have to initiate the self-destruct sequence."

When President Sharpe spoke, it was almost with a tone of defeat. "Copy, General. Quasar, vacate immediately."

"There's got to be some other way to do this!" Soren called out, but Bolton shouted over him.

"There isn't! Now get out of here! We haven't got time, and there's no sense in having more casualties!"

Soren obeyed reluctantly and fell back. President Sharpe spoke again. "All clear," was all she said, and Soren watched the Star Buster become an eight foot ball of flame in the center of the meteor. The rock and metal burst apart like a grenade in midair, fragments flying in all directions. A sonic wave rocked the atmosphere, and even with the distance between himself and the blast, Soren was nearly knocked out of the sky, ringing filling his ears. Even miles below them, dust was kicked up in waves from the explosion, and a handful of trees seemed to have bowed from the force. But the threat had been eliminated. Around the world, people would be cheering to the sound of the celestial firework that had just detonated.

Soren ducked and weaved through the pieces of the demolished meteor, looking for Bolton, hoping that perhaps, somehow, the military general would have survived the explosion.

When he found his target falling to Earth, he knew there was no chance of Bolton's survival. His body was charred and mangled. Gashes marked a large portion of his burned flesh. He was gone, and he wouldn't be coming back like Soren had.

He then slowly became aware of a voice that had been repeating in his ear. "Quasar, status update! Respond immediately! Qua—"

"I'm alright, Madam President," he said slowly. He snatched Bolton's lifeless body in his arms and began flying back toward Nevada. "The meteor is destroyed. I'll be back soon."

The comm channel was silent the rest of the

trip. Unlike when he had been deployed, he took a much more leisurely pace in returning to the base. It was midafternoon when he arrived to the applause of a detachment of military troops, but it hardly felt a time to celebrate. As the crowd realized what he was carrying, all fell silent, and President Sharpe approached.

She escorted him back inside the base, and a team of doctors took Bolton's body. Soren was given time to clean up, then arrangements were made for Bolton's funeral. It was to be at Arlington National Cemetery, and he was to receive a large number of posthumous honors. President Sharpe was quite heavily involved personally in the preparations, despite the protests of her advisors that there were more pressing matters.

And thus the preparations passed with Soren in a daze. He and Bolton hadn't exactly been close, but he had somehow formed a kind of bond with the general that made things feel empty, knowing now that he was gone forever. This time, unlike with Holst, he didn't have anger to pass onto someone else. Both of them had gone into the mission knowing either of them could die, yet the reality of it was stupefying nonetheless.

In a short time, Soren had been alienated from his old life and lost two people he knew. No, not just lost, but witnessed their deaths. Deaths that were, frankly, brutal. He felt as if he was watching life from outside his own body.

Then, too soon, yet somehow not soon enough, the funeral was upon them.

CHAPTER 13
HONORS

Arlington National Cemetery
Tuesday, August 31, 2027

Despite Bolton having no family, the funeral was massive. Senators, congressmen, and governors turned out. Battalions of United States troops stood shoulder-to-shoulder. News reporters commented on the happenings. Citizens crammed in to pay their respects. And various world leaders had arrived to thank President Sharpe for finding Soren and Bolton to protect the Earth.

Soren lost count of how many hands he shook or hugs he received. Everyone seemed to be craning their necks just to catch a glimpse of one of the men who had saved the world from destruction, and as the funeral was entirely closed-casket—Bolton's body could not be restored to a viewable state—they were all looking toward Soren.

For once, Soren detested the attention. It hardly seemed appropriate that he should be receiving this praise during a funeral. Though he admitted to himself that while Bolton's sacrifice was significant, his sadness for Bolton was nothing compared to the sorrow he had felt for Holst's loss.

At last, President Sharpe approached the podium that had been set up for her, and all fell silent. "Before we begin, I would like to thank you all for showing your support today," she said. "As you now know, two days ago, a meteor of the mineral called quasinium was due to collide with our planet and bring about global extinction. However, due to the valiant efforts of two men, this catastrophe was prevented. These men are Doctor Soren Grant and General Harold Bolton. They were successful in their mission, but at a cost.

"Both of these men behaved as heroes on a day that will undoubtedly go down in global history. Doctor Grant, who has since been known by the moniker 'Quasar', was, thankfully, able to return home alive. General Bolton, however, was not as fortunate. He gave his life that day to destroy that which would have otherwise destroyed us all, and for that, we owe him a debt that can never be repaid. For the actions of General Bolton, I now call for a national moment of silence in his memory."

At her command, even the birds seemed to have stopped their singing. The silence was invasive, and in those seconds of quiet, even to cough or to sneeze felt like it would be a capital offense. Heads were bowed and silent tears were left to their own devices. At last, President Sharpe's head lifted once more.

"Thank you," she began again. "General Bolton, as any who knew him well could tell you, was a patriot, through and through. So when he was asked to protect not just his nation, but his world, he answered the call with urgency…"

President Sharpe's speech went on, ensnaring the attention of all who listened. Not a soul said a word as she described Bolton's heroism and thanked him for his service. When at last she descended from the podium, her eyes were wet with tears.

Others took their own turns making speeches and giving thanks, and as noon came and went with many still saying their piece, Soren could not help but wonder how long it may last. Finally, at nearly two in the afternoon, the speeches ended.

Then it was time for the awards. Soren didn't recognize most of them, but was sure at least one of them was a service award that had been invented for Bolton's specific actions. He did, however, recognize the Purple Heart and Medal of Honor that were bestowed upon the late general.

Following this was the singing of "Amazing Grace" and a prayer, along with another moment of silence. Then a trumpet sounded, "Taps" echoing mournfully off the nearby trees. At last was the salute. As the twenty-one guns began their tribute, Soren knew it was time for the part he had been assigned. He launched into the air above the cemetery and put out a large amount of energy. As the guns sounded one after another, Soren hovered overhead, blazing as bright as the midday sun, his arms outstretched. New shadows were cast along the scene below as he shone, and as the guns ceased, and he descended back to the ground, his tribute complete.

The crowd began to dissipate as the casket was lowered into the ground. Soren followed the people's lead, but was stopped by President Sharpe. "Doctor Grant, I know I've asked much of you lately, but I have one last request before we part ways."

"What's that?" Soren asked, exhausted and looking to escape any further gawking or prodding.

"It's top secret. I cannot give you information here, but if you come with me, I can show you."

Soren agreed, wondering if he would ever be free from secrecy again where the President was concerned, and followed her to a stretched limousine flanked by a copious security detail. They were ushered inside by the driver, and it wasn't long before the car was moving.

CHAPTER 14
LODESTARS

Washington, D.C.
Tuesday, August 31, 2027

"I must ask before we reach our destination," President Sharpe said after she and Soren were in the privacy of the limousine, "do you, by chance, see yourself continuing in the hero business?"

"Business, ma'am?"

"Of course. You don't expect people to no longer need saving just because you stopped one meteor, do you?"

"I wouldn't imagine so," Soren said. "But I guess I had always thought of it as a lifestyle rather than a business. Have I got a choice to return to normal?"

"It would seem not from the analyses that have been performed on you," she replied. "Forgive me, but I have spent little time with you to know your values. While I do not like to look for the worst in people, it could be possible that your assistance in the incident on Sunday may have been for more selfish motives."

Soren pondered a moment. "It's true I was hesitant when Doctor Holst recommended taking up a heroic position in the world. But now, it would feel wrong to let others come to harm knowing I have the power to stop it."

Isolde smiled. "I had hoped you would say something to that affect. So you will undoubtedly require sustenance and housing, I am sure?"

"It would certainly be appreciated."

"What if I told you all you need could be provided by the government in exchange for your service?"

"Like, being a 'hero' could be a paid job, you mean?"

"In some capacity, yes," she acknowledged. "I'm aiming to locate more people of extraordinary talent like yourself. 'Superheroes', as some may call it. If successful, this could become similar to its own branch of the military. But I'm convinced after recent events that such a group of individuals may be necessary."

Soren looked skeptical. "With all due respect,

I'm not looking to be a soldier to fight your wars for you."

"Perhaps I misspoke. There may be threats, both within this world and without, that normal people will find themselves unable to defend against. It is for extraordinary threats that we must employ extraordinary defenses, such as yourself. That is my hope for you, and—in time—others like you."

"That," Soren said, "sounds a little more accurate to my expectations. But I'm still not sure why you needed me to tag along with you. Where are we going?"

"You'll see," she smirked. "We're almost there now."

They rounded another bend in the road and a large building came into view. It was a building of steel, glass, and concrete, but somehow it looked sleek and aesthetic even with simple materials. Above what appeared to be the main entrance was an emblem: a seven-pointed star, split into seven equal fragments and encased in a circle.

"Welcome to the Lodestar Compound," President Sharpe said.

"The what?"

"The Lodestar Compound," she repeated. "A location that is to serve simultaneously as a base and as living quarters for the heroes who join the organization. Collectively, any who join will be known as the Lodestars."

"Lodestars," Soren said, turning the thought over in his mind. "And you want me to be the first member?"

"Precisely," she said. "Or at least the first living member. Doctor Holst and General Bolton, due to their contributions, will be honored as members posthumously, of course. The building is home to the most state-of-the-art technology available. Automated doors, voice controlled security systems, dimmable windows, and holographic communications are just skimming the surface."

The car came to a halt, and they were ushered out. They stood side-by-side on the front patio of the building, looking up at the magnificent archway that formed the entrance. "So, will you accept?" President Sharpe asked.

"Count me in."

THUS BEGINS THE
TALE OF QUASAR....

ABOUT THE AUTHOR

Jesse Timm was born in Kankakee, Illinois, and has long been a fan of fantastical stories about heroes and villains, good versus evil, and saving the world. He holds a belief that one should do in life that which they are most passionate about, and with *QUASAR: STARBORN*—his first complete novella—he has accomplished that goal. Nowadays, he finds himself living in Trinidad, Colorado, and is looking forward to writing more stories in the *Lodestar Saga* and beyond.

A SNEAK PEEK AT

STAR BUSTER
INAUGURATION

PREVIEW
A NEW PATH

Washington, DC
Monday, September 4, 2028

All across America, the news was still buzzing: Isolde Sharpe—the first elected female President of the United States—would not be running for a second term in office. She had not given a reason, and speculations ran wild on the topic. Some believed she had perhaps fallen terminally ill, as she hadn't made a noteworthy public appearance in weeks. Others believed that the near catastrophic meteor impact from a year ago proved to be taxing to her mental health.

Yet the public remained in the dark as to her true reasons for removing herself from the presidential office. In reality, she had decided to take a more hands-on approach in the Lodestars, an organization she had founded to support and employ superhuman individuals. This, she surmised, would leave her unable to grant her best efforts to running a country.

The Lodestars yet remained a top-secret organization. Their members were few, beyond the hand-selected science team that dedicated their efforts to understanding such powerful individuals as Soren Grant, who had gained power of extraordinary proportions only just before the meteor event over a year ago, and none too soon at that.

The role she had hoped to fill was the pilot for the newest and most up-to-date model of Star Buster armor, a robotic suit designed to combat nuclear weapons and withstand their explosions. The most recent model of armor was smaller than its eight-foot-tall predecessors, instead able to automatically conform to the height of the wearer through autonomous modifications.

And it was in the basement of the Lodestar Compound that she was located at that moment. Joining her was Doctor Soren Grant—also known as Quasar. Together they directed the finishing touches for the new armor. In a short while, the Star Buster Gamma I would be ready for a test flight.

"Have you managed to track down a new pilot yet?" Doctor Grant asked. "It won't be long before the Star Buster will be ready."

"Yes," Isolde replied. "And no."

"I don't follow," Soren said, furrowing his brow.

"*I* will be the one to fly the Star Buster," she explained.

Soren recoiled. "You… you can't be serious right now. Putting on that suit could be tantamount to suicide! You could—"

"Be maimed? Killed? Perhaps worse?" she interrupted. "I'm aware of the risks, doctor. I was there when General Bolton gave his life to defend his country, nay, his planet. *I* made that call. Over the course of my presidency, I've issued commands while others fight my battles for me, both literal and figurative. A leader who hides while their followers die for them is no leader at all. Next time there needs to be another General Bolton, another sacrifice, it will be *my* life on the line, not someone else's."

"I still think you should reconsider," the doctor chimed.

"I've done all the considering I need, Doctor

Grant. A full year of it, in fact. As far as I'm concerned, this *is* the best course of action. And even if it's not," she paused, her expression both focused and pensive, "it's the road I'm going to take."

She stepped up to the suiting platform, where the armor stood open like a shed cicada skin, waiting for whomever would pilot it to step inside. A tester wearing a body glove was finishing his preparations for the test flight when Isolde's hand met his shoulder.

"You may stand down. I'll take things from here," she commanded.

"Madam President—"

"That's an order."

"Yes, Madam President."

She took a deep breath as she stared at the inside of the armor. She stepped out of her high heels and shivered as her toes met the cold steel of the metallic husk. She was stepping—both literally and figuratively—out of the shoes of a politician, and into the shoes of a warrior. She hesitated for only the briefest of moments—even she almost didn't notice. Then, both her feet were in place and the armor took the lead, closing around her. A helmet obscured her vision as she felt a jetpack settle in place over her back. Each limb was quickly encased in metal as she heard the sounds of the scientists—muffled due to the steely shell now firmly encasing her skull—beginning to panic in realization that the president had just entered the Star Buster Armor. Just as expected—just as designed—the armor had adjusted to her size perfectly.

Excitement and nervousness gripped her in ways she hadn't felt since taking the oath of office, and even that rush of emotion paled in comparison. Knowing no one would see past the chrome mask, she let herself smile—a rare occurrence for the usually quite formal and stern Isolde Sharpe. Once more, she trembled, but not from the cold this time. She had no real experience with the powers she was about to take on. No one could truly tell her what to expect. Unlike the presidency, where hundreds had preceded her, she was about to cut a path through the unknown.

Finally, the visor lit up, showing her the room in

front of her, accompanied by a heads-up display showing the amount of power remaining in the supply, fuel remaining in the jetpack, as well as the integrity of the shields and various pieces of the armor. Sounds from outside the suit were made audible to her via receptors built into the helm of the armor, amplified in such a way as to give her a crisper understanding of what was going on.

"Madam President," a scientist urged, "for your own safety, I must ask that you exit the Star Buster."

"I helped to draw the blueprints, doctor, and I've read all the manuals. I'm well aware of what I'm doing, more than most who would be in my shoes." As she spoke, the cables and robotic arms holding the armor in place disengaged. "If you don't mind, I'll be the one to perform the test flight this evening."

"Madam President, I must object—"

"I've been through this with other advisors already. My mind will not be swayed. Besides, if anything goes wrong, Quasar will be watching over me, correct, Doctor Grant?"

Soren came into her field of view, having shed the lab coat he had been wearing before and now displaying the specially designed suit that Isolde had gifted him with just over a year prior. "Of course, Madam President."

"Then if you would, doctors, open the hangar doors," she requested. After a moment of disgruntled shuffling on part of the scientists around her, a massive set of metallic industrial doors slid apart, a heavy hum of moving parts echoing throughout the chamber they stood in. Beyond was revealed a glowing cityscape framed with the stars of the night sky, yet inside the protective shell, the chill of the autumn night did not reach Isolde. She took another deep breath. Then, heat swelled in the jets on her back, and together she and Quasar rocketed into the night.

www.ingramcontent.com/pod-product-compliance
Lightning Source LLC
Chambersburg PA
CBHW060044150626
46556CB00018BA/2688